CONTENTS

The Goddess	3
Dedication	4
Chapter 1	5
Chapter 2	19
Chapter 3	33
Chapter 4	66
Chapter 5	83
Chapter 6	101
Chapter 7	114
Chapter 8	124
Chapter 9	140
Chapter 10	160
Epilogue	180
About the Author	196

THE GODDESS
Dave R.H.

DEDICATION

To Larry Poston, my friend and mentor. You have taught me lessons that I reflect on everyday of my life. I don't think I've ever told you how much you've taught me nor how much I appreciate it. Thank you for all that you have done.

DISCLAIMER

This story is a work of fiction. Any resemblance to person, place, events, etc. are purely coincidental. If any of you have experienced anything as fantastical as what is written here, please tell me because I would really like to know.

CHAPTER 1

The soft wind against her skin was enough for Kara to forget about everything. As she looked out at the waves of the cold arctic waters atop her horse, everything seemed right in the world. It felt like nothing could break this peace. Ever since she was a child, whenever things would be at its worst, sitting atop this cliff and watching the waves helped to ease her mind. A moments peace was all she wanted, and this spot never failed to deliver it to her, no matter how brief.

Her country lay behind her while the unknown ocean lay before. No one knew what lay beyond the waters she was looking out towards. Beyond the ice fields could be new lands, new peoples, new civilizations, or it could just be empty. It could just be a cold wasteland as so many others believed. She wondered if anyone was doing the same somewhere else. If there was someone in a far-off land looking towards her wondering the same thing.

"Kara, we should get back."

Kara's peace evaporated at the woman who had ridden up next to her. Her adopted sister, Delia, could hardly be called a woman at barely eighteen years. Kara wasn't much older at twenty-three but being heir to the throne forced her to mature faster than she or her father would've liked. Even if she weren't royalty, the state of the world at the moment had forced many young people to mature fast.

Delia was an abandoned orphan that was taken in by Kara's father, King Atlin. From the moment Delia had come into the royal palace, the two young girls were inseparable. Regardless of whether they were blood or not, they considered each other sisters and would gladly give their lives for one another. The people didn't think it proper for royalty to mingle with someone as low as an orphan. The priests especially made a big fuss. After all, Kara wasn't just royalty. Kara was the reincarnation of their God, Yalka. At least that was the excuse that people used. The reality was far different.

Before Kara was born, the priests had prophesied about the birth of Yalka.

At the sunrise of the new year, one day after the birth of our nation, Yalka will return to his people. He will be born of royal blood. He will lead them into greatness. He will bring great change. He will act as protector, guide, and commander. A new dawn will emerge for the people of Khalia.

King Atlin did indeed have a child one day after the new year. However, that child turned out to be a girl and Queen Arita died in childbirth. The people mourned the loss of their beloved queen and cursed the child born of her womb. The priests added fuel to the fire when they suggested the child should be killed. They claimed the birth of the child was a bad omen. They said the child was not the savior of the Khalian people. She was a curse. She would bring destruction to the nation and its people. That child turned out to be Kara.

It was only by the will of her father that Kara survived. King Atlin, being a decent man, was not about to allow the execution of a child, much less his own. He challenged any who would oppose him to raise up arms against him. No one dared challenge the king and thus, the young girl was spared the sword.

Growing up, Kara was always ostracized. In the land of Khalia, the royal family is not as separate from the people as in other lands. The country itself was quite small consisting of only three cities surrounded by farmland. In the capital city of Andor, the royal palace rests atop the highest hill. However, the people are permitted to enter its grounds and walk its halls. An audience with the king can be requested at will by any citizen. The king himself is known to walk through the city and mingle with the people. A common tradition for royal children was to live among the people for an extended amount of time in their youth. This was to allow the future leader to understand his subjects better. It was also during this time that Kara realized how deep people's resentment of her was.

Kara had resided in the palace until her twelfth year. Being an exceptionally bright child, Kara knew that her father was sheltering her from something. The priests would often look at her with a glare in their eyes. Citizens who visited the palace would whisper behind her back whenever they saw her. She didn't realize the extent of the hatred until she was placed with a merchant in the city.

Nobody had volunteered to take in the young princess. King Atlin had to call in a favor and that happened to be with a merchant named Gillard. The king had taken him in from a neighboring country called Anaya. Since immigration into Khalia was stringently regulated, Gillard considered himself lucky that he was allowed in. Not being a native of Khalia, he didn't share the fanatical religious beliefs of the masses. However, he understood taking the young girl in would affect his business. People didn't want to do business with the man who was sheltering the "devil's child." Not to mention, it would be another two extra mouths to feed since young Delia was permitted to accompany the princess. Still, the king was an old friend and Gillard had owed much to the man. Therefore, he couldn't refuse when the king asked the merchant to do this favor for him.

The city of Andor consisted of five rings. Each ring extended outward from the royal palace and was separated by stone walls. The main outer wall was the thickest and consisted of a single gate. Since Andor only had a population of about ten thousand, there wasn't much traffic for there to be more gates. Most of the people stayed within the city walls and the farmers outside the gates stayed within their fields. Andor was still the largest city in the country since the other two cities, Nabu and

Voya, only had around five thousand people each. Gillard had a hut in the first ring near the main gate.

The walk down to the hut from the main palace was eye opening for the young princess. Before Kara, Gillard, and Delia had left the fifth ring, someone threw urine at the poor girl and called her a whore. Gillard was able to rush his charges through the crowd and protect them to the best of his abilities, but the damage had already been done. Kara was in tears by the time they'd shut themselves inside the small hut.

King Atlin could do nothing but watch from the hilltop of the royal palace as his daughter was abused with insults. When he saw the man throw the cup of urine at his daughter, he seriously considered ordering the man to be executed. However, his friend and royal guard, General Gallus, put a hand on the king's shoulder and told him, "You knew this was going to happen."

It was true. The king had done everything he could to prepare his daughter for this. He taught her of the prophecy and the reasons why the people treated her the way they did. However, can you really prepare a child to actually face the reality of being hated?

Gillard put Kara to work with managing the shop. He wanted to limit the girl's interaction with the customers as much as possible – for both her safety and his business. Little Delia was put to work alongside her sister. She would help restock the shop and do any work her little body could handle. For the most part, they did exactly as any other merchant family in the city would do. Gillard even grew fond of the two young girls and treated them as his own. However, every once in a while, a customer would spot Kara and begin hurling insults at her. The worst were the teenage boys. They would come into the shop just to harass Kara. Gillard would chase them away quickly but not before leaving Kara in tears. Luckily, despite only being a child herself, it was little Delia who always knew what to say and do in order to ease her sister's pain.

King Atlin would visit the shop every single day regardless of how busy he was.

"You can come home. You can do this some other time. Maybe after a few more years." he would tell his daughter.

Despite the hardships, Kara would always say, "No. I have to do this."

Although it broke his heart to see his daughter suffer, King Atlin was proud of how strong she was. At such a young age, she was already showing the strength of her will. Still, as each day passed, the king could see his daughter slowly change. The constant trials were wearing the girl down and the king knew his daughter would never be the same after this experience.

After two years of living amongst those who hated her, Kara returned to the royal palace. Sure enough, the young girl had changed. She was no longer the child who pranced around the halls with a smile on her face. She was a young woman determined. Despite the hatred and the insults, she loved her people and she loved her country. A queen was not supposed to rule. She was meant to serve. She would serve her people even if they hated her. That was the promise she made, and she never forgot it.

"Kara, we really have to go. They're waiting for us."

Once more, Delia's voice broke the young woman's thoughts. Taking a deep breath, Kara looked out one last time at the expanse of water in front of her.

"Alright, I'm ready." Kara replied.

The two women turned their mounts around. Off in the distance, Kara could see Andor in all its splendor. Kara remembered the first time she saw Imbor. Imbor was the capital of the neighboring country of Anaya. Compared to Andor, Imbor was a technologically advanced metropolis. It boasted a population of two-hundred-thousand with a skyline more beautiful than anywhere else in the world. Kara was in absolute awe the first time she'd seen it. Her neck had been sore for a week from looking up at all the tall buildings. Still, there was nothing like seeing Andor. She couldn't explain it. There was just something about her home that made her heart swell up with emotions. It was quite ironic since the city held so many painful memories for her. Most of which were instigated by the very people that lived within its walls. Regardless, she would give her life for this city. It may very well come to that within the coming months.

****

Aurin sat on his mount watching as the two blurry figures moved closer towards him from the cliffs. He had been royal guard to the princess for only five years. The royal guard was the most esteemed position in the entire military. Once the heir to the throne turns eighteen, a royal guard is chosen from the ranks of the graduating class of the army. As was the case for Aurin, it's usually the soldier at the top of his class.

In Aurin's case there were two contenders to graduate at the top – himself and another named Gidor. It was no secret that Gidor held no love for the princess. He never believed the princess was Yalka incarnate. He also felt the princess was a spoiled little girl who would bring the country to ruin should she ever take power. It was expected that even if he were offered the position of royal guard, he would turn it down. However, he never got the chance. Aurin graduated ahead of his peer and was offered the position himself.

Aurin didn't know whether the princess was their god. After all, she never showed signs of having any supernatural abilities. She showed remarkable intelligence but nothing a learned person couldn't achieve. In fact, from the five years he'd spent with Kara, he doubted even she believed it. However, he completely disagreed with Gidor's notion that the princess was spoiled and incompetent. Instead he saw a woman who loved her people despite the scorn she suffered from them. She would willingly give her life for any one of them. She was also an incredible tactician and knew more than any of the officers in the army. If anyone took the time to actually get to know her, at the very least they would've gained some respect for the woman. Alas, the stigma she held was enough to keep people away. Even those who were forced to speak to her kept their distance.

Even if Aurin were one of these people who held Kara in contempt, he didn't have the luxury to keep his distance from her. The royal guard was assigned to the heir for life. Even as the royal guard was promoted through the ranks, he never left the side of his assignment. King Atlin's royal guard was General Gallus. Like Aurin, Gallus was assigned to Atlin when the king was but a prince. Gallus himself was only a mere twenty-two years. He continued to stay by the old king's side until one of them would eventually pass. From what Aurin understood, Gallus had never been less than twenty feet away from the king since he'd taken on his assignment. When the king awoke, Gallus was always there. When the king would empty his bowels, Gallus would stand by the door. Even when the king made love to the late Queen Arita, rumor had it that Gallus was in the room with them. Aurin knew the reality was that he stood outside in the doorway. However, Gallus was close enough that he could hear just about everything going on inside.

Aurin and Kara's relationship was somewhat different. Kara was the first female heir the kingdom had ever had since the inception of their nation 670 years ago. Even if the eldest was a girl, the king usually had multiple children and the heir would be a male. Therefore, Aurin would often give the young lady her privacy when she needed. Even if Kara had been a male, as independent as the young heir was, Aurin doubted he'd be able to guard her the way Gallus guarded her father.

The first few months being assigned to Kara were the worst. Kara never liked the idea of having someone following her around at all times. Whenever she would enter her room, Aurin would insist on going in first and making sure no one had put something in there to harm her. This meant going through her things including her undergarments. Needless to say, this didn't please the princess. Despite only doing his job, the icy glare the princess would give Aurin after events such as these would make him incredibly uncomfortable. It was the type of glare a woman gives to a man before she did something bad to him and all he can do is wait for it to happen and hope he doesn't suffer too badly.

Indeed, Aurin did suffer. Kara would make guarding her a living nightmare for him. She had an uncanny ability to get away from Aurin's protective gaze whenever she felt like it. One time in the markets, Aurin literally turned his head for a second to find the princess had run off somewhere. He literally started flipping stands over and making a scene trying to find out where she went. Kara appeared shortly thereafter laughing at her befuddled guard. She would also sneak off in the middle of the night and go riding in the city. Thankfully, the city at night was quite calm and the way the girl rode her mount was enough to wake anyone close by. Aurin only had to listen to the speeding hoofs of the horse to locate her. As swift as she was, it could still take hours to find the girl and when Aurin did, she acted like she'd done nothing wrong. Scenes like these were common until Aurin finally relented and begged the young princess to give him a break. Luckily, they came to an agreement where he would respect her privacy. In return, Kara would no longer sneak off whenever the whim took her.

The cliffs were an example of this agreement. At first, Aurin was a bit reluctant to let the princess go so close to the cliffs. The young girl liked to dismount her horse and hang her legs off the cliff's edge at times. However, he also knew how much Kara liked to spend time there. It was her place of peace and he wasn't going to take it away from her. He would always watch from a distance and let the girl have her own time. As long as she was in eye distance of him, he was doing his duty of guarding her.

The two blurry figures became clearer as they came closer to his position. He could make out the two hilts of the swords attached to Delia's back. He smiled to himself thinking about the young girl's predilection for the dual swords. As far as he knew, no one else fought with two swords. He knew that some warriors did so in other countries but in their own, soldiers tended to prefer the sword and shield or a single great sword. He himself preferred the great sword as his weapon of choice.

In fact, it was unusual for a woman to pick up arms at all in Khalia. Delia had never shown she was interested in warfare until after Kara left to study in Imbor. After Kara had turned sixteen, she was sent to Imbor to study under Master Grishom. For the first time, Delia was left alone without her sister. She was eleven at the time and growing into a young woman herself.

One day, she went out into the training yard where the new graduates were taught swordplay. She picked up a sword on the ground and began swinging away at one of the practice dummies. Her small frame and inexperience were not lost on some of the men who were there observing her. Not to mention the fact that she was a girl. They began mocking and laughing at her until the king alongside General Gallus came out and saw her.

"Get back to what you were doing!" Gallus ordered.

The men shut up immediately and ran off to their assignments. The king stood there and watched as Gallus grabbed another sword and approached the young girl.

"Hold your sword with two hands. Take a proper stance." he demonstrated to Delia.

Perhaps it was because Gallus saw some potential in the girl. Perhaps he didn't like the fact that the others were mocking her. Regardless of the reasons, it was the start of a long process of transforming this young girl into a fearsome warrior.

The king himself encouraged this by presenting the girl with a sword for her twelfth birthday. The greatswords in the yard were always too big for the girl to control properly. This new sword was made especially for her. The following year, Delia asked for an identical sword to compliment the one she already had. She began developing a style of her own, fighting with dual blades instead of one.

By the time Kara had returned two years later from her studies abroad, young Delia had grown quite proficient in swordplay. Kara herself was quite talented with the sword herself. Master Grishom in Imbor was tasked with teaching Kara the intricacies of diplomacy. However, the old warrior did more than that.

"Diplomacy is all well and good – when it works. When it doesn't, you have to be prepared to fight for what you want." the old man would say.

For Master Grishom, war was just another facet of the diplomatic game. He made sure Kara knew it as well.

As for Delia, her skills only improved with time. The mocking from the men ceased as soon as she proved she could best any one of them in combat. It's a known fact that Delia is the most skilled swordsman in the country. At only thirteen, she was able to defeat anyone to the point where the men refused to spar with her. Even Kara would get frustrated after suffering defeat after defeat. Despite being quite good herself, nothing Kara did seemed to work against the younger and smaller opponent. Delia truly was something special.

Yet, none will admit any of this out loud because of Delia's gender. To Delia, none of this mattered. She didn't care whether others acknowledged her skills or not. What mattered was she could beat them when she had to. Actions spoke louder than words and she prepared herself fanatically for when the time came.

The two women slowed and stopped their horses as they reached Aurin. Kara didn't even look at her royal guard. Instead, her eyes were focused towards the city and what awaited them there. Her peace was completely gone now, and it was time to come back to reality.

"You ready to go, princess?" Aurin asked.

Kara finally looked at Aurin as the question was asked. She couldn't help but shake her head every time he addressed her. She had asked him countless times to call her by name. He wasn't much older than her, being only four years her senior. Even if he were younger, Kara would still prefer to forgo the formalities. She hated being addressed as "princess", especially by those closest to her. She most certainly disdained being called a goddess although no one in the kingdom used that title unless they were insulting her. It was a reminder that she was a failure from the moment she was born. Instead of the god Yalka being born and fulfilling the prophecy, a "goddess" was born to bring ruin to the country. At least that was what the people of Khalia said.

Over the past five years, Kara and Aurin had developed a friendship. It was a friendship meant to last a lifetime. Although there was some tension between them at first, over the years, the two had become close. In fact, all three of them had become quite close. They shared laughs, pains, disappointments, and horrors. Kara could still remember six months ago in Imbor when she first saw the horrors of war. It was also the first time she saw the extent of the threat that lay before her own country and just how inadequately they were prepared to deal with it. Through it all, were her two closest friends. They were her family, and each would give their life for the other.

"I'm ready." Kara responded with a deep breath.

Kara gave a weak smile as she responded but Aurin knew it was a forced one. He saw quite a few of those in the past few months. Kara wanted to reassure her countrymen that everything was fine. She wanted to appear strong and be the leader her people needed her to be. However, Aurin knew better. He had seen the juggernaut approaching. It had already decimated their neighbors and were now coming for them. Anyone who could properly smile after seeing that was either insane or delusional in the thought that anything could survive it.

All three riders took one last deep breath of the fresh air away from the city. They turned their horses and began riding towards the gates at a moderate pace. There was no need to push the horses just now and none of them really wanted to get back to the city anytime soon.

"You think they'll make a decision on anything today?" Delia asked, breaking the silence.

"It's a war council. What do you think?" Kara responded sarcastically.

The three of them laughed together but just like the smiles, it was a forced laugh. The sad reality was that the council had met twelve times in the past three months. This was unprecedented in the history of the nation. The war council usually met once a year to discuss the state of the army and any changes that might be implemented. In 670 years, there had only been three major changes. The first was the organization of the army into what it is today. The second was the introduction of a material called iron and how it could benefit the army if fashioned into weapons and armor. Finally, there was the construction of the all powerful Khalian navy. This last idea consisted of three outdated ships during its peak. The Khalian navy today still had those three ships from a hundred years ago. Only two of which were still operational and docked indefinitely in the shipyard at Andor. Basically, in nearly seven centuries, not much had changed. Khalia moved at its own slow pace and the military was no different.

Even though the war council frantically met several times over the past few months, they rarely came to any meaningful decisions. Everyone had their own idea of how to best handle the threat coming for them. King Atlin himself was powerless to do anything. Despite being trained to use a sword during his youth, he had no military experience. Neither had any of the generals on the council for that matter. The only ones who had seen actual war were the three young riders now headed towards the city. No one listened to Kara because it was believed any of her suggestions could lead them to destruction. No one listened to Delia since she was an eighteen-year-old child and a woman on top of it. Aurin was never even permitted to speak. He was only in the room because his place was to protect the princess.

There were ten generals on the war council including General Gallus. Also invited to the meeting was Archbishop Tula – the spiritual leader of the Khalian people. He made his opinion on Kara known long ago when he was the first person to suggest she be executed moments after birth. Being of the clergy, he never even held a sword before. Many on the council wondered if his presence was even necessary, especially since he seemed to instigate many of the disagreements. However, the Khalians were a deeply religious people so representation from the church was deemed necessary, especially in times of crisis. Thus, the war council usually came down to a bunch of incompetent generals and one ornery priest arguing amongst themselves until exhaustion set in and they decided to close the meeting.

Near the city walls, the three passed by the military training fields. All men in the nation of Khalia were required to undergo military training once they turned eighteen. For the first two years, the young boys, some of which had never been away from home, weren't even allowed to pick up a sword. They were trained in traditional Khalian martial arts, often implementing a wooden staff. It was only in the final two years of their mandatory service that they were given swords and shields. Even then, they weren't taught much other than how to properly hold their equipment.

The sounds of men training filled the ears of the three and Kara couldn't help but shake her head. All this was such a waste of time and effort. For four years, the men weren't taught a thing about actual warfare. It was only after the four years that a graduating soldier could choose to be a career soldier. Career soldiers were moved to the training yard near the royal palace. This is when they would be taught actual warfare tactics. Unfortunately, even these tactics were outdated.

Kara once brought up this inefficiency to the war council only to be shot down immediately. She was told it was tradition and in Khalia, no one messes with tradition. It didn't help that the "devil's child" was the one who suggested forgoing tradition for practicality. Kara had different theory for why the military training was structured this way. It wasn't a secret that when the military was established, Khalia was not as united as the current day. The kings of those days were probably afraid of being overthrown by their own people. Therefore, the military only trained those loyal to the crown how to actually fight, while giving the rest of the people the illusion that they were being trained as well. Of course, nobody would ever admit to this. As far as the Khalians were concerned, they had never been divided, and everything was just the way it was for past six-hundred-seventy years since their founding.

As the three rode their horses, Aurin could feel the speed from the other two riders getting slower and slower as they approached the walls. He really couldn't blame them. Nobody wanted to be at the meetings. In fact, General Gallus himself spent the last meeting with his elbows propped on the table and his face buried in his hands. He could've sworn the old man was asleep for most of it.

"Maybe it'll be different this time." Aurin said.

The three exchanged looks before bursting into laughter. This time it was a legitimate laugh, although not very hearty. The reason for their laugh was quite sad. The idea that the council would get anything done was preposterous. Still, they needed the laughter.

"Come on. Let's get there before we walk in late and they decide its reason enough to execute me." Kara said.

Aurin was just glad he could put a smile on the faces of his friends. His duty as a royal guard was to protect the princess until death. His duty as a person was to enrich the lives of his friends. He took his duties very seriously.

CHAPTER 2

General Bellus looked out over the Yandu river in front of him. The men had been busy fording the river, day and night, for the past two months. The river was narrow and shallow. Too shallow for any of the massive ships of the Numeran navy to navigate. Thus, the only way across was to ford it and allow for the army to march across. It would only be a few more days now. A few more days and the final battles of the massive campaign to conquer the world would begin.

As Bellus looked out over the land, he couldn't help but scoff. Khalia was an ugly land. It was the most northern part of the world and only consisted of three cities. The entire country made up only about twenty-thousand people. The Khalians isolated themselves from the rest of the world. Their only foreign relations were with their neighboring country, Anaya. It had only been a few months since Anaya had become part of Numera. Now, Khalia stood alone and no one was coming to aid them. It wouldn't have helped anyway. Every nation had fallen under the might of the Numeran Empire.

If the Khalians only knew the truth about the birth of their nation, they probably would have cut themselves off even further. The Anayans had kept meticulous records over the course of their history. Apparently, almost 700 years ago, Anaya became embroiled in a civil war. Those that lost were exiled out of the nation and left to die a slow death in the wasteland that was now Khalia. However, the Khalians thrived and were able to survive the harsh conditions of their new home. They established the nation Bellus was now looking out at.

Of course, this was history that was lost to the Khalians

themselves. If they knew this, they would probably harbor some type of resentment towards their neighbors. That's what characterized the Khalians. They were stubborn and set in their old ways. So stubborn in fact that the harsh conditions of the north couldn't even kill them. On some level, Bellus actually admired that. On another, he equated them with roaches. No matter what you do, they just keep coming back. However, none of that mattered now. Anaya was gone and soon Khalia would join their neighbors.

A cold wind blew across the landscape making Bellus shiver in his armor. He ran his hands through his horse's mane to keep warm. Light snowflakes began coming down. It had begun to snow again, and this would delay the fording of the river further. Bellus grunted in displeasure and one look around would indicate that the rest of his men felt the same.

The only thing moderately good to come out of this land was a sweet vegetable called sapa. It grew out of the ground and looked like a beet but tasted like an apple. The Khalians farmed it because it was the only thing that could grow in this godforsaken wasteland. The country was too cold to grow anything else. Every city was surrounded by sapa farms. The Khalians would trade with Anaya for other goods, even meat. Being so desolate, meat was hard to come by in this nation. The army found that out the hard way. Bellus himself hadn't had any decent food for the past few weeks. Since Numera had cut off Khalia's trade with Anaya, the Khalians had to be going hungry as well. At least that was the hope.

Bellus wasn't stupid. He knew that even an enemy as weak as this could prove to be challenging. He had no doubts Numera would succeed in the end but at what cost? How many of his men would have to die for this garbage heap? Taking Anaya wasn't easy. It had cost the lives of thousands of his men. So much in fact, that they had to wait for reinforcements from the south before marching on Khalia. If there was anything Bellus could do to limit any casualties, he would do it.

There was one other thing Bellus was concerned about.

It was the fact that the Khalians were deeply religious. Bellus had fought against religious fanatics before. Years ago, when he was but a captain in the infantry, Numera conquered a people known as the Traya. They were hardly a nation. It was a dozen tribes which would come together in times of war. They believed their gods inhabited the warriors and gave them supernatural abilities. It was all superstition and garbage but the Trayans themselves fought with religious zeal. Zealots were always tough to fight and from what Bellus understood, the Khalians were quite fanatic about their religion.

Apparently, the worship of the god Yalka is older than Khalia itself. In fact, the entire world once worshipped Yalka. Over time, the belief in Yalka faded only to be replaced by a pantheon of religious gods and idols. Bellus himself never adhered to any of this superstitious nonsense. Every time a city would be on the verge of conquest, the inhabitants would pray to their gods for salvation. None ever answered and the people were either enslaved or slaughtered. If there were any gods out there, Bellus was sure they feared Numera rather than the other way around.

The Khalians were somewhat different though because of the living heir to the throne. Apparently, there was some girl who was considered to be the reincarnation of Yalka. Bellus couldn't help but scoff at the contradiction. Yalka was supposed to be a man. Yet, you have this girl barely out of her teens claiming to have fulfilled a prophecy? The contradiction wasn't lost on the Khalian people either from what Bellus understood. Most of them considered her to be the "devil's child." It didn't help that their beloved queen died giving birth to the religious disappointment.

Bellus had actually seen this alleged "goddess" on the walls of Imbor six months back. Anaya had asked Khalia for military support in repelling the Numeran invasion. All Anaya got were a hundred men and the goddess. It was hysterically sad. In fact, the entire army burst into laughter when they saw the pathetic excuse that was intended to be aid. The Numeran army had already laid siege to the city by the time the Khalians had arrived. The young "goddess" used the cover of night as well as an ingenious distraction to sneak past the Numeran camps and enter the city. By the time the Numerans had realized what had happened, the Khalians were already being let into the gates. Upon seeing the pathetic force, Bellus decided to let them enter and be slaughtered with their allies rather than risk approaching the walls. He did have to give the girl some credit. She was clearly intelligent enough to sneak past all the patrols. However, when the fate of the city was sealed, he saw the little bitch run with the handful of her men that still survived.

Therefore, Bellus wasn't too worried about this supposed "goddess" or the Khalians rallying behind her. If anything, she was a liability for the Khalians. They might just blame her for all the misfortune that befalls them in the coming months and kill her themselves.

The real threat in Bellus' mind was the goddess' sister. Bellus had only recently learned the girl's name, Delia. She had cut down dozens of Numerans during the Battle of Imbor. The small Anayan force which defended the city seemed to rally behind this girl. If she could inspire the same type of zeal within the Khalians, it could lead to a real problem.

Bellus caught sight of a young messenger running towards his horse. The boy was out of breath and leaving small prints in the freshly fallen snow. Every breath the boy took could be seen as if he were breathing out smoke. It was another testament to how cold it was in the north.

"General, word from the scouts!" the boy announced.

Bellus couldn't help but look down at the boy and smile. He reminded Bellus of when he was that age and had first joined the Numeran army. Emperor Gradus had come into power only five years earlier. It had only taken Gradus a year to mobilize an army to conquer the Southern Alliance. The Alliance was made up of four independent nations who would band together in times of war. These dark-skinned people were incredibly advanced, and their coffers were full. Their conquest would enrich Numera and lead to further prosperity.

Unfortunately for the southern peoples, they had not seen war for generations. They focused more on trade and scientific advancements. Not to mention, this "alliance", had degraded over time. When Numera crossed their borders, they spent their days arguing instead of coming together like they had in the past. Everything from who should lead the main army to where they should focus their defenses were a subject of debate. All the while, Numera pillaged and burned city after city. By the time the southern peoples became single-minded enough to put up any type of resistance, it only came down to two nations – the other two having capitulated already. Even this "resistance" could hardly be called that. Despite their scientific advancements, they'd put none of it towards warfare. While Numera attacked them with steel weapons and formations, the Alliance charged at them in a disorderly fashion brandishing arms they had scrounged up from their grandfathers' closets.

It was only four years after the complete subjugation of the Southern Alliance that a young boy from the Numeran capital of Bella decided to join the army. Gradus' campaign was unprecedented in the history of the world. He aimed to conquer more than the neighbors on his border, he wanted it all. Everything from the southern oceans to the northern arctic. Therefore, he needed men. Fortunately, Numera had the largest population of any country. In Bella alone, there were 500,000 inhabitants. The overpopulation was one of the reasons why Numera was in such dire straits before Gradus came into power. The conquests emptied the city of poverty-stricken individuals and provided for them in the army. Those who were left could provide industry for the war machine. At the same time, the plunder from the conquered would enrich the nation. War wasn't a choice for Numera, it was a necessity.

Bellus himself was a poor orphan boy trying to survive on the streets. When the message went out across the nation that every able-bodied man was obligated to join the army, it was a relief for the young boy. He would finally receive three square meals a day, receive the best military training in the nation, and have a sense of belonging. Bellus began his service as small pathetic eighteen-year-old child. As with most orphans in the nation, he was quite small for his age due to malnourishment. However, within two shorts years, Bellus was a trained killing machine along with the rest of the young men in his company.

Bellus began as a foot soldier and was sent straight to the frontline. Truth be told, he didn't even know who he was fighting. All he cared about was killing the men on the other side. They were in Numera's way to greatness. Either they would put down their arms and surrender or be run over, trampled, and spit on.

Whenever Numera sacked a village or city, the surrendering soldiers would either be executed or pressed into service for Numera. Usually it was the former since the allegiance of foreign soldiers were considered to be a liability. The last thing you wanted was for these newly conquered conscripts to turn on those fighting alongside them in the midst of a battle. However, as Numera continued to spread further away from the home nation, it became necessary to replenish lost forces quickly instead of waiting for reinforcements from home. The civilian inhabitants were pressed into "service" as well but in reality, it was slavery. The men were pressed into the army or taken back to Numera to work menial labor. The children were sent to Numera to be sold on the slave markets. The women had it the worst. Some were sent to the slave markets back in Numera but most of the time, they were at the mercy of the soldiers looking for "female companionship." Within the military camps, a third of the population were women from conquered nations. They were considered the property of the soldiers who owned them.

Over the years, Bellus had seen several of his friends and comrades die in combat, usually at the incompetent orders of those in charge. Bellus was promoted to General only three years ago at the start of the Anayan campaign. He made it a priority to keep as many of his men alive as possible by limiting decisions which put his men in harm's way. Unfortunately, this didn't always turn out the way he wanted.

Everyone knew the Anayans would not fall quickly. They were considered the most powerful nation in the world other than Numera. It took a full three years before their entire nation fell. Throughout it all, the Emperor would get impatient at times with how slowly the conquest was going. He would order Bellus to speed things up which usually meant taking risks and making decisions which cost lives. It was only then that Bellus realized his anger might have been misdirected at the officers above him. Perhaps he should've been aiming it elsewhere – at the Emperor himself.

As more time went by, the more Bellus was torn over this. He knew that without Gradus, Numera would be a downtrodden joke of a nation to the rest of the world. He also knew that he would either be dead or still be picking up scraps off the streets. He felt he owed much to the Emperor. At the same time, he'd often seen Gradus show complete disregard for the men in the army, to the point of using them as playthings. Bellus once witnessed Gradus order two companies forward just to soak up the arrows of the opposition. It had worked. Once the defending army expelled their arrows onto the advancing companies, they were left with just their swords and spears. Four-hundred Numerans were killed for no other reason than to act as fodder and Bellus never forgot it.

Bellus considered himself lucky to have survived all these years. Looking down at the young messenger boy in front of him, he wondered just how long the boy would last if Emperor Gradus continued giving the orders.

"What's the word?" Bellus asked the boy.

"General, the scouts have found a passage through the mountains as you ordered. They're on their way back now." the boy responded.

Bellus smiled at the welcoming news. The Khalians believed that the only way into their nation was across the Yandu river. Therefore, they were focusing their defenses on the city of Voya which was directly north of the river. However, to the west was the city of Nabu. It bordered the Karisian mountains and the Khalians believed there was no way across it. The scouts had found a way though. Bellus' plan was to send a force across those mountains and take Nabu by surprise. By then, the river would be forded, and the main army could march on Voya. Afterwards, both the eastern and western forces could converge on the capital of Andor together.

"Something else, General." the boy added.

"What is it?" Bellus asked.

"The Emperor summons you, sir. He awaits at the main camp."

Bellus' smile turned into a grimace. Whenever the Emperor would summon him, it meant he was becoming impatient again. Bellus was actually surprised it took this long for the man to call for him. Over the past six months, Bellus was concerned that the Emperor would order the men to swim across the river or some such stupidity.

With a deep sigh, Bellus told the boy, "Send word that I'll be there soon."

"Yes, General!" the boy saluted and ran off.

Bellus breathed out one last long breath into the cold air before turning his horse around towards the main camp.

Let's go see what our bloodthirsty leader wants. he thought to himself.

****

The Emperor had his tent in the middle of the main army camp. However, he spent most of his time atop his portable throne. The throne was a large steel platform with a seat on top. At all times, the throne was carried on the backs of one hundred slaves, separated into rows and columns of ten. These men and women were worked to death. They were not fed, washed, or given any basics of life. From the moment they were assigned to carry the throne, it was a death sentence. Even when the

Emperor was not sitting upon the throne, the slaves would be tasked with carrying it. The eight imperial guards surrounding the throne made sure of that.

When Bellus arrived, the Emperor was sitting atop this death contraption sipping wine from a goblet. The Emperor was in full armor at all times. It was black as night and richly adorned. The black and red cloak behind him contrasted with the material, making him seem majestic. The helmet itself had horns coming out of the sides to curl up and meet at the top of its head. This made the already tall man seem even more imposing. No one knew who created this armor except for the Emperor. Rumor had it, Gradus had the man killed shortly after making it so that he could not duplicate it for anyone else. Bellus didn't know if the rumors were true but he wouldn't put it past the man.

Bellus bowed his head and saluted atop his horse as he greeted the Emperor.

"I come as summoned, Your Imperial Majesty." Bellus said.

Bellus remained in this position until spoken to. Even though the Emperor was not donning his helmet at the moment, he still looked intimidating. Bellus always had trouble making eye contact with the man. The Emperor had the eyes of a man who knew he had power and wouldn't hesitate to use it. Gradus was a man who was sure of himself. He didn't believe he could lose nor was there anyone who could stop him from getting what he wanted. He was the most dangerous type of man. To look this man in the eyes was to look at a predator in the eyes and dare him to come eat you.

"What is the status of the fording, General? I am getting impatient with the delays." Gradus bellowed.

The Emperor's voice was deep. It shook most people to the core when they heard it. Even if this man had no power at all, his voice alone would've been enough to stay the hand of anyone looking to attack him. This was another reason Bellus tried to avoid the Emperor. Whenever he spoke, Bellus felt like the Emperor would order his execution with the next sentence.

"Apologies, Majesty. The main attack on Voya will occur soon. In the meantime, the scouts have found a path through the Karisian mountains. The attack on Nabu can proceed as early as this week." Bellus reported.

"It's about time." Gradus said calmly.

Bellus was relieved to have appeased the Emperor for the time being. That relief was interrupted by the sound of metal stomping on the ground from behind him.

"Let me lead this attack on Nabu, Majesty!"

Bellus turned to see where this intrusion had come from only to regret it. It was Decimus, the greatest warrior of Numera.

If there was anyone who could match Gradus' bloodlust, it was Decimus. The man was almost eight feet tall. He made even the Emperor look small in comparison. Truth be told, Bellus wasn't even sure if Decimus was a man. He never took off his armor and no one had even seen his face. The men claimed he was some type of demon. Although Bellus had never been superstitious, he could believe the rumors after seeing the cruelty inflicted by Decimus against his enemies.

Decimus had a belt around his waist. On this belt were sharp hooks which held the tongues of the champions he'd slain. In each major battle, Decimus would challenge the greatest of their warriors. Obviously, he triumphed over every single one up to this point. Decimus would always wound the champion instead of killing him. It was at this point Decimus would proceed to remove the man's tongue while he was still alive. The final screams of their champion before his tongue was torn out would demoralize the opposition. There were times when entire armies would surrender immediately after witnessing this heinous act of cruelty. Of course, Decimus would always keep the trophy by hooking it onto his belt. He already had twenty-four such trophies and looked to gather more.

"Looking to add more tongues to your collection, Decimus?" Gradus asked.

"As always!" Decimus replied as he extended his wrist blade.

The wrist blade was Decimus' weapon of choice when he cut the tongues out of his victims. The blade shot out from the top of his gauntlet and was nearly four feet in length. He didn't use this blade just for the cruel act he enjoyed. Bellus had witnessed how Decimus would expertly manipulate his opponents with this weapon. Such a thing would not have been possible for a normal sized soldier. It was testament to the strength and skill of this man.

"Very well. Leave no one alive." Gradus said.

"Your will!" Decimus replied in satisfaction before marching off.

Bellus was actually glad to be spared at least one battle in which he wouldn't have to hear the screams of Decimus' victim. Although Bellus was no stranger to war and violence, he also was not a man who reveled in cruelty like most of the men in the army. In fact, whenever a city was sacked and the men were busy raping, looting, and slaughtering, Bellus would never partake. He realized it was the victor's right to do as they pleased to the conquered. However, Bellus just never took pleasure in such things. Cruelty, in and of itself was gut-wrenching for Bellus. Of course, he never told this to anyone else lest they perceive him as weak.

"Plan the attack, General. Do not disappoint me." Gradus ordered.

"As you will, Majesty." Bellus replied with a bow.

As Bellus turned to leave, one of the slaves holding the platform fell to the ground in exhaustion. Those around him grimaced as they struggled to hold the platform steady.

Don't stumble! Bellus thought.

Wobbling the platform was a death sentence for all one hundred slaves underneath it. They would be taken away to be tortured and crucified. The genitals of the men would be cut off and the breasts of the women would be removed before they were hung on a cross to be left to die. The lucky ones would bleed to death quickly. Some may have already been on the cusp of death due to exhaustion so they might even pass while the mutilation was happening. The great majority would be unlucky and left to suffer an agonizing death which could take hours.

Slaves holding the platform would die every single day. No one could hold the heavy platform without rest for more than a day before succumbing to exhaustion. Therefore, there were literally thousands of slaves dedicated to just this one task. Bellus understood they were just slaves, but it was such a waste of resources. These slaves could be put to work fording the river or some other task. Many of them were taken from conquered nations, thus they were educated. They could improve the camp and the Empire as a whole in other ways.

Luckily, in this case, the slaves maintained their balance. The one who fell tried to quickly get up and recover but he had already committed a cardinal sin. As the imperial guards came for him, the man began begging for his life.

"Please! I won't fall again! Spare me, I beg you!" he screamed.

The man was dragged, kicking and screaming towards the front, in view of all the other slaves. He was to be an example of what happens when you fall. Bellus shut his eyes as the royal guards began hacking his limbs off. When all four limbs had been removed, he was left there to bleed to death. It was less of an example of failure and more of an example of what awaited all of them. They all eventually fell. No one could defeat exhaustion.

The removal of the limbs was another brilliant idea by the cruel Emperor. There had been incidents in the past where a slave would feign exhaustion to escape their fate. When the throne was first created, this happened quite often, especially when the throne would be on the move. A slave would collapse, and everyone would continue to move on. They would leave the slave for dead but if the slave was feigning, they could just get up and run away. The Emperor realized this and began ordering the slaves to be amputated. It gave the slaves more incentive to work harder before dying as well as preventing any malingerers from escaping.

Some had doubts about this plan. Bellus himself felt that some of these slaves might prefer a painful yet quick death rather than suffering for a prolonged time before meeting the same death regardless. Even had anyone questioned the Emperor, Bellus doubted Gradus would've listened. The Emperor seemed to revel in the screams of the suffering. There were times Bellus had seen the man almost jump for joy when another slave collapsed. If anyone did have the courage to question the Emperor about this, there was a good chance they would share in this cruel form of execution.

Bellus turned to leave, but once again he was given pause. The new slave that came to take the place of the man who was killed was brought in. She was Anayan by the looks of her. Her golden hair and blue eyes gave her ethnicity away. Nowhere else on the continent did people have such characteristics besides the newly conquered nation. She was also not as emaciated and disheveled as the others. The men took especially good care of the Anayan women due to their beauty and instilled elegance. The men wanted something clean and pretty to ravage after a long day of duty. It was clear to Bellus why this one was here though instead of in some soldier's tent.

The girl was pregnant. She was showing a significant bump in her belly. There was no telling how many men had their way with her thus far and clearly no way of even guessing who the father might be. From just observing her, she had probably conceived six months ago when Imbor was sacked. Her eyes were red and bloodshot with tear stains streaming down her face. She already knew the fate she in for.

As the girl was pushed into position, Bellus called out, "Wait!"

Everyone stopped and turned towards Bellus. Even the Emperor's eyes were on him.

"I want that one." he indicated to the girl.

This surprised everyone including Gradus. Bellus was known for not taking any slaves to his tent. Yet, he now wanted one who was pregnant.

Gradus chuckled and said, "I must say, Bellus, I've never known you to take a slave woman to your bed."

"They were never pregnant. I like pregnant women." Bellus replied. "Would you deny your general this, Your Majesty?"

The truth was, Bellus didn't like pregnant women or any women at all. He preferred the company of men. He had kept this a secret because this was also seen as a weakness within Numera. Men who laid with other men were considered to be weak. This perception had always been the case, long before Gradus even came to power. Of course, the same stigma didn't apply to women. Women were already considered as being weak, so it didn't matter if they wanted to lay with other women and weaken themselves further.

"Not at all. Have your fun." Gradus replied.

"I thank you, Majesty." Bellus replied with a bow.

The girl was taken by some soldiers towards Bellus' tent. As the two made eye contact, Bellus could see the gratefulness in the girl's face.

She's just a slave. Bellus thought.

Yet, he wondered why he cared so much. He had cared enough to risk the Emperor's anger.

CHAPTER 3

Six Months Ago...

The siege had been going on for two months now. So far, there had been no major battles. From the hill where Kara was at, she could see that the entire city of Imbor was surrounded by the Numeran camp. Along the Eastern Sea, which Imbor bordered, the Numeran navy had set up a blockade to stop any reinforcements or supplies from Khalia. The last vestige of Anaya was cut off and alone. The only aid that would be arriving were the one hundred men Kara had brought along with her. They had each been hand-picked and had no problems with taking orders from Kara. Every one of them were career soldiers and well-trained. The problem was, none of them had ever seen real warfare.

It had taken everything to convince the war council to allow Kara to take the one hundred men. The council only granted Kara's request because the girl was relentless. It got to the point of sheer annoyance and some of them were even hoping she'd be killed in this conflict. Archbishop Tula was ironically the voice that eventually allowed Kara to aid the Anayans. However, Tula didn't do this for philanthropic reasons. Tula knew that no matter how this turned out, he could spin it to promote his own agenda. The best-case scenario was that Kara would be killed in the battle and Tula would be rid a powerful enemy. Even if Kara survived, there was no way she would emerge victorious. Losses would be sustained by Khalia and Tula knew he could exploit the grievances for the fallen. He could lay the blame on Kara and her "devilish" ways.

This fact wasn't lost on Kara. In fact, everyone in the

council knew what Tula was up to. For Kara, it didn't matter. What mattered was that she got the men she requested and permission from the war council to proceed. Anaya would get the help it requested no matter how small and insignificant it might seem.

Now, looking at the Numeran camp in front of them, even Kara's faith was shaken. There were thousands of them. They looked like a sea of black ants swarming over a freshly dropped sweet. Just getting past them towards the gate would be a significant hurdle. If they could even get in, fighting this swarm off seemed next to impossible.

Kara looked back down the hill to where her men were taking the time to rest. It had taken them eight days at full gallop to get here as quickly as possible. These were all the horses Khalia could muster. The country was too cold to keep a large number of mounts at hand. As valuable as they were, every plan formulating in the young woman's mind told her to leave the horses behind. There was no way to sneak past the camp while the hooves of one hundred horses stomped across the ground.

As Kara looked out over the enemy camp one last time, Delia and Aurin rode up next to her. Kara breathed a sigh of relief at the presence of her two closest friends.

"Aurin, I thought you were giving me my space for a while." Kara teased.

"I got lonely." Aurin replied sarcastically.

This incited a chuckle from Delia. Kara was surprised the girl could bring herself to laugh after seeing the sight in front of her.

Guess for the best warrior in Khalia, this is just another evening. Kara thought.

In truth, Delia was terrified. Despite being the best, she was had never seen combat either. Delia knew she could die during this battle and laughing was the only thing keeping her sane.

"Do the Anayans know we're coming?" Aurin asked.

"If the Anayans can see us, the Numerans sure as hell can." Kara replied. "Seeing as how we aren't being charged by the Numeran cavalry, I'd say no."

"Well, we better find a way to get the Anayans' attention. It'd be pretty stupid to approach the gates only to be shot by their archers." Delia said.

The Anayans had the best archers in the world. While most archers in other countries were trained to saturate an area with arrows, Anayans were trained to aim carefully. It was said that every Anayan arrow fired would hit a target. Whether you survived being struck was either luck or how strong your armor was. It was also the reason why the Numerans hadn't attacked yet. Of all the military casualties the Numerans had suffered during this campaign, more than half of them were due to Anayan archers.

Kara had once proposed the idea to the war council of training archers for their own army only to be scoffed at. The Khalians always considered archers to be cowards. They attacked from range and refused to face their enemies in "honorable combat." Kara knew archers were essential to winning battles, especially from a defensive standpoint. The Anayans had lasted three years against the Numerans, longer than any other country, because they had the best archers. Archers gave the attackers pause, giving the defenders the extra time to formulate new plans. They also whittled down the enemy numbers before melee combat commenced. It was foolhardy to think like the Khalians did but in Khalia tradition was everything.

As the three friends stared out into the Numeran camp, Delia and Aurin began to come to the same conclusion Kara had earlier.

"We're going to have to leave the horses, aren't we? Aurin asked rhetorically.

As Kara was about to relent and give an affirmative answer, she saw a sight that put a smile on her face.

"Not if we're smart. We'll have to be fast. Oh, and we'll have to risk getting shot." Kara said.

Delia sighed and said, "I hate this plan already."

****

As night fell, Kara could feel her heart beating out of her chest in anticipation. Either this plan was going to work, or they would all be slaughtered before entering the city – quite possibly by the very people they were trying to aid.

Delia finished hooking up the device to her horse. She had grown fond of the horse she'd named Ella and hated to do this to her. Unfortunately, it had to be Delia's horse. Delia was the smallest and lightest out of all of them. She could ride with Kara and be light enough that it didn't hinder their speed. If they didn't get through the Numeran camp fast enough, they wouldn't even have to worry about the second part of their plan. They'd all be dead.

The device was meant to trail behind the horse and release oil when she ran. The Numerans would most likely kill her once they realized what was going on, but it was a sacrifice they had to make. The alternative was to leave all the horses behind and try to sneak in on foot. The horses would either die from the elements or worse, be used by the Numerans against the Khalians in a future campaign.

With one last deep breath, Kara looked over at Delia and nodded.

"Sorry, girl. If it makes you feel any better, we'll probably join you soon." Delia told Ella.

Delia lit the oil behind the horse and smacked its rear. The horse whinnied at the sudden jolt and raced off towards the Numeran camp. Delia climbed onto the back of Kara's horse as Kara gave the signal to raise their banner. Their hope was that the Anayans would see the banner flying high and recognize them as friendlies long before they reached the gates. Otherwise, this plan could end in disaster. Everyone's eyes were focused on Ella. Kara swore the only sound she heard were the beating hearts in her men's chests.

Ella ran straight into the stable area of the Numeran camp where their horses were kept. Some of the Numeran guards stood frozen in place at the sight before them. There was a horse literally leaving trails of fire behind it as if it were some supernatural entity. The fire had done its job and the other horses began to panic. Some of them broke out of their pens and began running through the camp. Ella had run out of places to go. When she turned around, she saw the trail of fire she had left behind. She began to buck and panic as well, causing the device attached to her to fly around, throwing fire and oil all over the place.

The plan had worked better than Kara had hoped. She felt bad for the horse, but the alternative would've been worse. The Numeran camp went into a panic and all the patrols moved towards the fire to help put it out. This was the moment the Khalians were waiting for.

"Now!" Kara screamed.

The one hundred riders roared down the hillside towards the wall. Kara at the vanguard led her riders towards the least occupied path. The sounds of the fire, men screaming, and the horses panicking on the Numeran side covered their own horses' thunderous stomps. The few Numerans who were in the way of the Khalians didn't know what was going on. All they knew was that there was fire and commotion on the other side of the camp. Most assumed the Khalians were their own cavalrymen trying to get their horses away from the flames.

As the Khalians passed through the camp, Kara breathed out a sigh of relief. Delia who was hanging onto Kara felt her sister breathe out and shouted, "It's not over yet!"

Delia couldn't have been more right as arrows began slamming into the ground near their position.

"Shields!" Kara screamed.

The Khalians raised their shields to block the incoming projectiles. Unfortunately, the Khalians found out just how outdated their military equipment was. The steel-tipped arrows the Anayans were shooting at them were punching through the iron shields the Khalians were wielding. One rider's horse took an arrow to the throat dropping them both to the ground. Kara looked back and was relieved to see another rider pick the man up and continue towards the gate.

"Wave the goddamn banner!" Kara shouted.

The banner bearer began waving the banner to get the attention of the Anayans. For all his efforts, the banner was soon riddled with holes from the arrows. The plan was turning into a mess fast, so Kara decided to act faster. She spurred her horse, racing ahead of the other riders.

All those nights sneaking off to race in the city were worth something now. Kara thought to herself.

As soon as she got to the gates, she began shouting, "Stop firing! We're Khalians!"

Still the arrows rained down. Despite the combination of both Kara and Delia screaming together, the Anayans seemed to be deaf to their pleas.

The girls were soon joined by the other riders and they all began shouting for the hail of arrows to stop.

"Son of a bitch!" one rider screamed as he took an arrow to the shoulder.

"Cease fire!" a shout came from the walls.

Soon, a horn sounded followed by another. Multiple shouts calling for an immediate cease fire began echoing along the walls.

Looking at her men, Kara could see the relief on each of their faces. Some of the men had two riders on them. Clearly, their horses weren't as lucky. Which begged the question as to how they got so lucky in the first place. Despite it being night, Kara could clearly see the outlines of the horses dead on the field. However, she couldn't see anything resembling that of men. Could they have been so lucky that everyone in her company survived?

She would get a proper headcount later. At the moment, the Anayans were raising the metal gate to their city. Kara and Delia stayed outside and made sure everyone entered the city safely. The men were relieved that it was over and comforted with the thought of being behind the thick walls of Imbor despite it being surrounded by the enemy. As Kara turned her horse around after the last man had gone in, she could hear what sounded like laughter in the distance. She looked back to see the Numerans looking right at them and laughing.

"Just what the hell are they laughing at?" Kara asked.

"Probably us killing each other. Or failing to do so. Take your pick." Delia replied.

As Kara and Delia rode into the city, they caught sight of Aurin. He was sitting atop of his horse waiting for them, as ready to protect as ever.

****

Bellus awoke to the sounds of commotion from the camp. He grabbed his sword and headed outside to see what was happening. The first thing he saw was fire engulfing the southern section of the camp where the stables were.

"Report!" Bellus shouted.

The men were running around in a panic. Some were moving towards the fire while others were running away from it. No one seemed to know what was going on.

The idiocy that runs in this camp. he thought.

Bellus grabbed a random soldier as he ran towards the commotion. By the insignia on his armor, Bellus could see that he was a private.

"What's going on?" Bellus demanded.

"General! There's a fire in the stables!" the young man replied.

"Obviously!" Bellus shouted in anger.

He couldn't believe the stupidity of the answer. A blind fool could've told him that.

"That's all I know for now, General!"

Bellus let go of the boy and started heading in the direction of the fire. He saw a captain standing there watching as the men tried to control the flames.

"Captain! What the hell is going on?" Bellus shouted.

"Everything is under control, General. Just a little fire."

the captain responded calmly.

"How did it start?"

"We don't know, sir."

Bellus felt like unsheathing his sword and cutting the man's head off for being so stupid.

"You don't know?! You idiot! Did it occur to you that this could be a counter-offensive?"

The captain's relaxed composure suddenly shifted to one of panic. Obviously, the thought didn't occur to him and Bellus wondered once again how a moron such as this could've become a captain in the first place.

Just then, a messenger ran up to the two officers and said, "General! There are reports of cavalrymen on the northern side of the camp!"

Bellus glared at the captain next to him before shouting, "Wake the men! Prepare for battle!"

The captain, along with several officers near enough to hear, began doing as the General ordered. Bellus went back to his tent in order to get his armor on. He didn't know for certain if the Anayans were responsible for this. For all he knew, this could've just been an accident. It would cost the guards on watch dearly, but it wouldn't be a cause for alarm. Still, if the Anayans were responsible, he had to give them some credit. He didn't think they had any will to put up a decent defense, much less go on the offensive.

As Bellus finished donning the last piece of his armor, he heard laughter arising from the camp. Upon exiting his tent, Bellus was dumbfounded by what he was looking at. There were several men on horseback at the front of Imbor's gate. They had arrows raining down on them whilst pleading to be let in. The banner which was torn to shreds was still identifiable as being Khalian. Bellus couldn't help himself as he burst into laughter. He didn't know what was funnier. The size of the Khalian reinforcements or the fact that the Anayans were having trouble killing this pathetic lot.

As the gates rose and the Khalians were being let in, his

smile faded at the sight of the woman staring right in his direction. He knew who the woman was through reputation. She had finally entered the field of battle. Bellus couldn't let an opportunity like this pass. Bellus grabbed a messenger and told him to take word to the Emperor. This so called "goddess" was in the city. The Battle of Imbor would begin in the morning.

****

"98... 99... 100." Kara counted.

Kara couldn't believe it. As soon as she and her riders entered the city, she took an immediate count of her men and assessed the casualties. Besides a few scrapes and bruises from falling off the horses and an arrow to the shoulder, all of her men had survived the approach to the walls of Imbor. A man came down the stairs leading to the upper wall. He was followed by two young boys, their armor too big for their small stature.

This man who was leading them was tall and grizzled. He had the look of a veteran who had seen many battles. Despite the darkness, Kara could still make out the darkness of his hair as well as his tan complexion. It was uncharacteristic for an Anayan. The Anayans usually had long golden hair and fair white skin aided by the use of cosmetics. Even the men paid close attention to their outward appearance, even in times of war. The Anayans believed that if they died in battle, they would meet their ancestors in the other world. Therefore, they always made sure they looked nice before taking to the battlefield. As the man approached and spoke, Kara was now positive this man came was from elsewhere.

"You made one hell of an entrance." he said.

Kara couldn't quite place his accent. It sounded like he was from Anaya's neighboring country of Sarina. The Sarinans and Anayans always had a close relationship. Sarina was known for its mercenaries. During times of war, Anaya would often hire mercenaries from this country to guard key locations. While the main Anayan army pushed forward, the Sarinan mercenaries would keep order in areas that had been captured. Knowing this, the Numerans attacked Sarina first. Despite hiring themselves out as mercenaries, the Sarinans lacked a central command for their men. Thus, they fell within weeks, long before Anaya could organize a force to come to their aid. It also forced Anaya to take the defensive in a war for the first time in their history. Their centuries old military doctrine in shambles, the Anayans began falling back until all that was left was Imbor.

"My name is Kara, heir to the Khalian throne. I've come with aid from my father, King Atlin." Kara announced.

The man looked around at the one hundred men who were recovering from their ordeal at the walls.

"Come with me." the man said.

Kara was actually surprised the man didn't say anything else. She knew the aid she brought with her was pathetic compared to what awaited them beyond the walls. She had expected the man to say something in regards to this. Regardless, Kara followed the man as he headed back to the stairs to the upper wall. Delia and Aurin followed close behind.

"My name is Nema." the man introduced himself as they walked.

"You don't sound Anayan." Kara said.

"Nor look it, I'd wager." Nema added.

"Sarinan?"

Nema chuckled and said, "I see the princess of Khalia is well versed."

"Are you in command here?"

This time Nema laughed aloud before saying, "I suppose. Although rank isn't really a high priority at the moment. Survival is."

As the company reached the top of the walls, the three Khalians froze at the sight before them. The reason why all one hundred of the Khalian riders had made it safely into the walls wasn't because of luck. The Anayans defending the walls weren't soldiers, they were children. There was barely anyone over eighteen years. Boys and girls, some of which could barely hold the weapon they were given were sitting along the walls shivering. Their armor looked like it was forged from whatever pottery was lying around the city. Half of them looked sick, vomit covered the floors of the wall, all of them were malnourished.

"What the hell is this?" Delia broke the silence.

"Ah, you see now why you survived the approach to the walls." Nema said. "Some of them only learned how to use a bow this afternoon."

Kara closed her eyes and breathed deep. She had no idea how desperate the situation was. It was clear why Nema hadn't said anything about the small force that had come to aid them. The Khalians were probably the only real warriors Nema had seen in a while.

"Where are all the soldiers?" Aurin asked.

Nema laughed as he spread his arms indicating to those around him.

"You're looking at them."

"I meant the Anayan army." Aurin said.

"Oh, you mean the actual trained warriors." Nema said sarcastically. "According to them, resting peacefully with their ancestors."

"All of them?" Kara asked in shock.

"Some of them might be alive. Hiding in some dank cave." Nema answered.

"Why are there only children?" Delia asked.

"Because the adults were drafted a long time ago. Anyone of eighteen years was drafted into the military. There are a few who turned eighteen when the siege first started but you couldn't really call them adults." Nema explained.

"Where's the king?" Kara asked.

The king should've been in the royal palace. As far as Kara was concerned, he should've been on the walls with them. Nema didn't say a word. He just pointed out towards the field at the center of the main camp. Kara looked out and saw the Numeran banner flying high. Through the darkness, she could see something on top of the pole. It took a minute to realize it was a human head. Not just any head, but one crowned.

"If you were thinking the king was a coward who hid in his palace, he was not." Nema explained. "He led his entire palace household against the Numeran camp about a week ago. The royal guards, the servants, even the dogs. He was trying to break the lines so that some of the elderly and children could escape. Didn't work out."

"Great. There isn't even an heir to the throne." Delia said.

The king of Anaya was a young man who had inherited the throne from his father four years before. Only a year after his coronation, Numera began their invasion. This didn't leave much time for the king to find a woman to make his queen. His focus was on repelling the invading forces terrorizing his country. Now, with the death of the king, the Anayan royal bloodline was lost.

Kara looked over at her two friends. They knew the truth as well as she did. Everyone in the city knew the truth. There was no way they could fight off the force in front of them. The Numerans would breach the city, kill anyone who resisted, and enslave the rest.

"As royal guard, I should advise the princess to leave." Aurin said.

Kara just looked at Aurin without saying a word. She didn't need to say anything. Her answer was written on her face. She would not abandon these people. If she died here, she would die fighting alongside them.

Aurin exhaled loudly and said, "I thought so."

Just then, everyone noticed movement in the camp. Even some of the defenders who were sitting silently stood up to look. Dawn was only a few hours away and the Numerans were preparing.

"Battle formations. So, it begins." Nema stated.

"What do our forces look like?" Kara asked.

"Everyone who can hold a weapon is on the walls." Nema answered. "The children under five and the elderly are down in the city. I can't give you an accurate count. Besides, would it matter? They're all untrained children who have been drafted into a war they shouldn't be fighting."

"Well then, we'll just have to make the most of it." Kara said.

"There is some good news though. We have eight ballistae arranged throughout the length of the wall. We don't have many bolts, but they could prove useful against the Numeran siege towers." Nema added.

"Can we expect their navy to attack?"

"Not likely. Right now, they're positioned to blockade any ships from entering or leaving the city. If they break formation, they risk our smaller ships escaping through the gaps."

This was good news. Imbor didn't have a wall protecting their eastern side since it bordered the sea. If the Numeran navy did decide to use their ships, the defending forces would be crushed between the navy on the east and army on the west.

"Let's hope they hold their positions." Kara said.

The war chants from the Numeran camp were now rising into the air. Fear struck the hearts of the Anayans within the walls. This was the moment they had been dreading for the past two months. For many of them, it would be the last few hours of life.

Kara knew they couldn't win. However, they could make it hurt. Whatever pain they could cause to Numera would be well worth it. It may even buy some time for Khalia to prepare their own defenses.

Kara looked over at her sister and said, "Delia, go downstairs and prepare the men. We're going to be in hell in a few hours."

****

General Bellus assessed the battle formations from atop his mount. As the first rays of the day's sunshine began to peak across the horizon, the full strength of the Numeran army came into view. Two-hundred-thousand strong were set to attack the greatest city in the world. Bellus only hoped the Numeran casualties would be low. Despite the main army being made up of men from various conquered nations, most of them were still Numeran. As far as Bellus was concerned, all conquered nations were part of Numera now and he was going to limit casualties wherever he could.

Each company was led a captain. They were speaking with their men now, trying to get them motivated for the coming conflict. The entire battlefield was echoing with the roars from the men. Bellus would stay at the rear and give commands as the battle progressed. Out of the corner of his eye, Bellus saw the Emperor's throne approach. Bellus' heart sank knowing that the Emperor would be there.

There goes the chance for low casualties. Bellus thought.

Bellus rode over to the Emperor's position, knowing the man would want a report.

"Your Majesty! It's an honor to have you on the field." Bellus lied.

"Report, General!" Gradus bellowed.

"Everything is going according to plan. We should be ready to attack within a few minutes."

"Excellent! Kill all who resist. Capture the rest."

"As you command, Majesty."

If Bellus could have it his way, he would've sieged the city a bit longer. The entire city was cut off and starving them out would've been preferable. This would have limited the Numeran casualties while at the same time, the number of captured would increase. The captured could be slaves or used as recruits to bolster their own forces. However, the presence of the goddess changed all this. Bellus didn't know if the girl had some supernatural ability or not. Of course, he didn't believe she did, but he couldn't take that risk.

The only blessing to attacking this soon was the fact that Decimus was not around. Decimus was still hunting down the few remnants of the surviving Anayan army to the south. He was due to arrive at the siege within a week and Bellus wasn't too keen on the idea of having him around. Decimus' very presence made Bellus uncomfortable. Not only that but Decimus followed no one's orders. He was given authority by the Emperor himself to do as he wished. Sometimes, Bellus found his entire strategy at jeopardy because Decimus could not control his bloodlust. An example of this was the Battle of Nessa eight months earlier.

Nessa was a small city in southern Anaya. It only had a population of around seventy-thousand people. This was a small number compared to the other cities within the country. Bellus' plan was to draw out the main force defending the city. Out in the open field, the Numerans could make quick work of the Anayans. However, Decimus had other ideas. Decimus took his small company of two hundred men and directly attacked the walls. Bellus had no other choice but to send in support for the men being massacred by the archers. Although Numera emerged victorious in the end, the casualties were in the thousands. Of course, all Decimus was concerned with was the fact he added another tongue to his collection.

Decimus would be upset he missed this battle. He would probably even take it out on some of his men. Decimus would often maim or kill the men in his company whenever he grew angry with something. Although unfortunate, Bellus felt it was better than the number of casualties they would suffer if Decimus were here now.

As the last of the companies marched into position, Bellus assessed the battlefield one last time. He had planned everything to the letter and prepared for any surprises. The only thing he was unsure about was the goddess. It made him nervous that there was an unknown factor on the battlefield. He had always maintained control over every aspect of a battle before commencing. Still, this was not an opportunity he could ignore.

Bellus looked at his lieutenant who held the signal horn. Bellus nodded to the man to commence the attack. The lieutenant blew into his horn, the sound filling the air and drowning out the chants, roars, and bustling of the men. Almost immediately, the sound of two-hundred-thousand men picking up their shields and marching in unison began to pound through the earth.

"Here we go." Bellus whispered to himself.

****

Waiting was the most excruciating part for Kara. She imagined the others felt the same way. As the morning sun began to rise, the time to battle drew nearer and nearer. As the Numerans lined up for battle, part of her wanted to fire a ballista bolt right into the middle of it. The men were lined up close enough to the walls for it to hit, and it would definitely give some pause to the enemy. They wouldn't risk continuing to line up while ballista bolts fell all around them. However, she also knew they only had a limited number of bolts. They would have to be used sparingly and against the siege towers. It would be a waste to fire it into the formation just to kill two or three men at a time while several thousand others continued to line up.

Nema seemed just as antsy as her. The man kept pacing back and forth while looking out towards the horizon. It actually started to get annoying to Kara. She wished he would just stand still.

"You never told me how you ended up here. You're a long way from Sarina." Kara said hoping the man would stop for a second.

Luckily, the man did and answered, "Fought for the Anayans after Sarina was conquered. I was in a battle four months ago where I got this."

Nema removed his helmet to show a massive scar on the top of his head. Kara winced at the sight. She was surprised the man was still alive to tell the tale.

Nema continued, "Long story short, someone brought me to Imbor to heal. Never found out who it was. I woke up two months later to find the city under siege. Turns out, I was the only veteran in the city. Since I had the most experience, they put me in charge."

To Kara's annoyance, the man started pacing again. She was about to tell him to sit still when a horn blasted through the air. With a loud roar, the Numerans began to march forward.

"Alright! This is it!" Nema bellowed to the defenders. "No matter what they throw at you, remember you are men and women of Anaya! You fight for your home, your country, your families!"

Everyone along the walls drew their bows, ready to fire at the oncoming army. Kara's own men were spread out along the walls. She knew they were spread thin. Imbor was a huge city and one hundred men weren't sufficient to cover the entire length. Delia had separated the men into groups of five and put them into equal sections. Since the Khalians were the only "real" soldiers, the hope was that they could add some much needed support to the Anayan defenders. Kara, along with Delia and Aurin, were in the middle of the wall where the main gate was. The fiercest fighting was expected to be here, and Kara hoped their fiercest warrior, Delia, would be enough to hold the line.

Kara turned to Delia and asked, "You ready?"

For the first time, Delia looked incredibly nervous. She let out a deep breath and said, "Yeah. Love you, sis."

"Love you too." Kara told her.

Aurin interrupted the touching moment by sarcastically saying, "Well, no need to say anything to me."

The two girls chuckled as Kara said, "You're right. There isn't any need. You already know."

The three friends smiled at each other knowing this could be the last time they might ever do so.

The defenders were shaking in fear as the army got within range of their arrows. Although some of them could barely hold their bows steady, the first wave of arrows flew away and pounded into the enemies' shields. Unfortunately, it didn't do much damage, if any. The Numerans were in tight formation and their large five-foot shields absorbed any projectiles fired at them. As the Numerans reached the base of the wall, they raised their shields to protect themselves as well as the ladders moving towards the front of the formation.

Kara observed a man hanging onto the top of the ladder as it was in the process of being raised. She realized this particular soldier intended to come up immediately as the ladder was raised. The Numerans called these men berserkers. They were heavily armored and carried a large battle axe. Berserkers were renowned for the fact that they were brutal and showed no fear. When a ladder was hoisted, they acted as the vanguard. They would go up with the ladder and clear the top of a wall so that the rest of the army could come up safely. Despite being such a dangerous job, their brutality alone made them incredibly effective.

As Nema got ready to order another volley of arrows, Kara screamed, "Hold fire!"

Kara knew these Anayan defenders were not trained archers. They were firing their arrows wildly and were only effective as a group.

"Aim for the Numeran coming up with the ladder!" she ordered.

Nema didn't object to having his order overridden. In fact, he realized what Kara was doing and let her take the lead. It was actually somewhat of a relief for Nema. He was a mercenary, not a leader. He never wanted to be in the position to command and now felt a bit reassured that this girl seemed to know what she was doing. As the ladder came up, the berserker on top got ready to pounce on the defenders.

"Fire now!" Kara screamed.

Multiple arrows flew at the berserker. Despite his heavy armor, the berserker was not prepared for this response. About a dozen steel-tipped arrows slammed into his chest as he lost his grip on the ladder and fell over thirty feet onto the men below him.

"Fire another volley now!" Kara ordered.

The men below were stunned when the heavy berserker fell on top of them. Some of them had dropped their shields and the formation broke while they scurried to right themselves. Before they could recover, a volley of arrows slammed into them. Multiple men dropped, causing panic amongst the ranks. The Anayans continued to fire into the broken formation, wounding and killing dozens more before a captain moved forward and restored order.

Looking around, Kara could see that the other defenders along the walls did not use the same tactic she did. The berserkers were on the walls cutting down the Anayans. Following them, the soldiers from below began storming the walls as well. Things were already getting out of hand quickly.

Another ladder came up where Kara was. This time, the berserker at the top was holding a shield. He'd obviously seen his comrade from before meet a bad fate and didn't feel like sharing in it. Regardless, the Anayans continued to fire at him. The shield the berserker was holding was riddled with arrows by the time he touched down onto the top of the wall. He immediately slammed the shield into a young boy, killing him instantly from the force alone. Delia ran over quickly and used her speed against the slow lumbering giant. She got behind him and sank her dual swords into his back before he could even turn around.

The Numerans began coming up the ladder as Kara drew her own sword. All the training she'd received from Master Grishom as well as the countless hours she'd spent sparring Delia were worth something now. Despite never having fought together, Kara and Aurin fought as if they were one. Each Numeran that came up the ladder was cut down by the duo quickly. However, there were more ladders coming up and too many Numerans for them to handle alone.

Nema and the Anayan defenders did what they could but the one warrior that really shone bright was Delia. Her reputation as the best warrior in Khalia was well deserved. The speed at which the tiny girl moved was almost inhuman. She dodged the Numeran attacks as if she were floating on air, gracefully coming down with her own strikes as she skillfully dispatched each attacker. To say that she made warfare look like an art would have been an understatement. It was more like magic. Watching her move and fight would have put anyone under a spell. Several Numerans stood there and just watched as the girl moved about killing anyone who got in her way. Before these men knew it, the girl had moved close to them and had somehow struck them with her swords. Most of these men died before they even hit the ground.

Seeing Delia inspired the Anayans to fight harder. Many of them began to feel as if they could actually win with this remarkable warrior on their side. Amazingly, the defenders began to rally, and word began to spread across the wall that the Numerans were being held back.

As Kara cut down her last man, she looked around to see the other sections of the wall clearing. Just then, she heard a horn blown from the Numeran camp. The Numerans on the wall began to climb back down the ladders. The few Numerans who were too slow in their retreat were cut down by the Anayans. The Numerans remained at the base of the wall but they were no longer climbing the ladders. Despite all odds, the Anayans had held the wall.

Kara couldn't believe it as a cheer rang out along the wall. The battle was far from over, but this group of untrained children had done the impossible. They had already lasted longer than anyone had predicted. For the first time, they had hope.

****

The ladders were not working and Bellus knew it. He stared at the center section of the wall where the goddess had taken position. From where Bellus was observing the battle, he could see his men being cut down as they got to the top. What was interesting was that there seemed to be another female with the young goddess. Bellus had no idea who she was, but she was an exceptional warrior. From the red hair on top of this girl's head, she was definitely Khalian.

"Lieutenant, call a retreat." Bellus ordered.

The lieutenant immediately blew into his horn as the remaining men retreated from the top of the wall. The army held its position at the base, but the ladders were becoming too costly. Bellus also did not account for this new warrior. He assumed the Anayans would rally around the goddess. Instead they seemed to be rallying around this warrior girl who was cutting down his men at ease. He needed to know who she was. Bellus grabbed a messenger and told him to retrieve one of the captains.

"That did not go too well, General." Gradus said as he sipped wine from his goblet.

"No, Your Majesty. It did not." Bellus confirmed.

"This does not bode well for you. You're being embarrassed by some girl." Gradus said with a chuckle.

Bellus grimaced at the thought. Over the course of the Anayan campaign, Bellus had seen multiple women fight for Anaya. However, none ever proved to be a challenge for the men. Numera believed women to be weak and not suited for war. Nothing Bellus had seen thus far was contrary to that belief. However, this Khalian woman was changing his opinion.

"The battle is just beginning, Your Majesty." Bellus said.

"Perhaps we should invite some of the Khalian women to bolster your ranks. It seems to be working for the Anayans." Gradus said as he laughed at his own joke.

Bellus' hope was that the defenders would be too demoralized to even fight off the initial wave of attackers. Apparently, this wasn't the case. This battle was going to take much more effort than he'd hoped. As Bellus began forming another plan in his mind, one of the company captains reached his position.

The captain saluted and announced, "General! I come as commanded!"

"Who's the girl?" Bellus bluntly asked.

Bellus didn't want to waste any time on formalities. He was already embarrassed enough as it was. The Emperor had only rubbed salt on the wound with his little quip earlier about inviting Khalian women into the ranks.

"The goddess, sir!" the captain answered.

Bellus got off his horse in a fury. He grabbed the captain by the neck and turned him towards the center wall. The goddess stood there looking at them along with the young woman who had thoroughly embarrassed him and his men.

"Not her you idiot! The other one!" Bellus yelled into the man's ear.

The captain struggled to get out of Bellus' grip but couldn't move.

"We're not sure, General. Some of the men heard the Anayans talking. They think she's the goddess' sister." the captain answered through his struggles.

Bellus threw the man onto the ground before turning around and getting back onto his horse. Bellus wasn't aware the goddess had a sister. Could the Numeran intelligence be mistaken? Could the goddess be referring to this younger girl? Bellus doubted it. Numera had a spy within Khalia. All the reports stated that the goddess was a twenty-three-year old heir to the throne. This other girl wasn't even out of her teens. There were also detailed descriptions of the goddess' appearance. The older one fit this description to the letter. There was no doubt as to who the goddess was. Which meant this young warrior girl was just a wild card in the Khalian deck. In the end, it wouldn't matter. Both girls would be dead before the sunset.

"Prepare the siege towers. Move them forward." Bellus told his lieutenant.

The lieutenant blew into his horn once again. Now, the massive wheels of the siege towers began to squeak and role across the ground. The towers were already full of the best men in the army. Once the ramps dropped on top of the walls, the end would come.

****

The onslaught had stopped for the moment. For the defenders, they needed to use this time to reorganize and treat their wounded. Although the Anayans had rallied behind the efforts of Delia, they had suffered numerous casualties. There was only so much they could do against a better armed and trained opponent.

Kara moved about trying to separate the defenders who could fight and those who needed to be evacuated. A boy no older than fifteen had his entire left arm severed. He had wrapped a tourniquet around his wound as he held onto his sword with his right hand.

Kara tapped him on the should to get his attention and told him, "Fall back to the royal palace."

"I still have an arm left, Your Highness." he replied.

Kara had to admire the boy. Even on the verge of death, he refused to abandon his friends. She knew he wouldn't be very effective when the second wave came but even if he fell back to the royal palace, it wouldn't have mattered. Looking towards the city, she realized the citizens who had taken shelter at the royal palace had come out to attend to their brave defenders. Men and women too old to fight, even children barely old enough to run, came with water and healing aids.

The boy's show of courage wasn't an isolated incident. All around Kara, the wounded refused to leave the walls. They knew the second wave would most likely be the end, but they weren't going to fall without a fight. The Anayans truly were a noble and courageous people.

Kara had sent Delia to get a report from her own men. She saw her younger sister run up to her and hoped for some good news.

When Delia reached Kara's position, all the girl said was, "54."

Kara didn't know whether that meant fifty-four were alive or dead. Kara didn't want to know. Either way, half the men were gone.

As the defenders recovered, they also pushed the dead bodies of both ally and fallen off the walls. The corpses made it too cluttered on the walls to fight properly. The last thing anyone needed was to trip over a corpse lying on the ground while having a sword swung at them. It pained the defenders to throw the bodies of their loved ones over the sides, but it was necessary. The Numerans at the base of the wall were horrified as the dead of both friend and foe were dropped on top of their heads.

As Kara grabbed the legs of a Numeran, she tossed the man over the side with the help of Nema. Although the man was an enemy, she couldn't help but feel sickened by the act. He was still a man. Surely, he couldn't have wanted to die in a foreign land for a cause he probably didn't care for. It made Kara wonder. How many of these men were here because they wanted to be? Kara was willing to bet that it probably wasn't many. How many of them were dying because of one man's vanity?

The once white stone walls of Imbor were now soaked in red. It was as if someone had poured buckets of paint on them. The blood ran down the sides in a macabre fashion. It reminded Kara of the ghost stories she'd heard as a child. Those stories always managed to give her nightmares when she was younger. Now, as an adult, new nightmares would invade her sleep. She longed to go back to simpler times when the only disturbing thoughts that invaded her dreams were those of specters and phantoms.

Just as the last few bodies were being cleared, the Numeran sounded the horn again. This time, the defenders could see the massive siege towers in the distance. The wheels thundered across the ground as the towers were pushed towards the wall.

Here we go again. Kara thought as she exhaled deeply.

"Get ready for the second wave!" Nema shouted.

Truthfully, Nema didn't have to say a thing. Everyone saw the second wave approaching and were rushing to get ready for it. For all they knew, this could be the end for them.

"Get the ballista ready!" Kara ordered.

Kara took position next to the ballista on top of the main gate. The defenders operating it quickly loaded a massive six-foot steel-tipped bolt into the machine. They took aim at the massive siege tower heading in their direction. The ballista team waited for the order to fire along with the seven ballistae positioned along the other sections of the wall.

Kara waited for the siege towers to get closer. The rhythmic chanting from the men pushing the large war machine echoed throughout the battlefield. The battle drums beat loudly and the men inside the towers roared with anticipation.

"Fire!" Kara screamed.

The first bolt flew straight and with such force that it tore through the siege tower. The unlucky few inside who were struck died instantly. The bolt itself slammed into the ground behind the tower, killing a few of the men on the ground. All around the wall, the other ballistae began firing as well. Unfortunately, the bolts didn't do too much damage. Despite having enough force to punch through the towers, the damage was superficial. The towers just kept coming.

"Again!" Kara ordered.

Within minutes, the ballista was loaded again and fired. Once again, Numeran screams filled the air as the titanic bolt crashed through the large wooden structure. Despite two large holes in the tower, it was still operational. The ballista team had time to load one last round.

"Wait!" Kara called out.

Kara had one last idea to try to stop to this tower.

"Aim directly at the ramp." she told the team.

The tower stopped as it made contact with the wall. The defenders anxiously waited for the tower to spew forth its deadly payload of armed men.

As the ramp dropped, Kara screamed, "Fire!"

The final bolt tore through the open ramp, piercing through anyone standing in its way. The Numeran veterans who had eagerly been anticipating their participation in the battle were stunned at the sudden attack. Instead of moving forward as the ramp dropped, they scurried about, trying to recover from their confusion. Kara took the opportunity to jump into the ramp herself as she hacked away at the men inside.

"Kara!" Aurin yelled as he tried to get to his charge.

Some of the Numerans inside the tower jumped onto the walls as they attempted to escape the commotion within. They were quickly cut down by the Anayan defenders, but this also prevented Aurin from getting closer to Kara.

"Delia, get to Kara!" Aurin yelled.

Delia moved quickly but she was surrounded herself by this point. General Bellus had spread word amongst the men that a special reward awaited anyone who killed the red-headed warrior girl. Delia was a prime target and the men began going after her specifically. Multiple Numerans attacked Delia at once. The girl was able to dispatch them, but it slowed her down in her attempts to get to Kara's position.

Kara didn't jump onto the siege tower on a whim. She had seen a weakness as the last bolt crashed through the structure. She made straight for it as she cut down any in her path. She began cutting and kicking at the weakened support inside the tower as the Numerans scrambled around her. Some were still trying to recover from being surprised by the ballista while others were trying to get onto the walls. Most didn't even see the young woman right next to them until the support finally gave way and snapped. With a sickening creak, the wooden tower began to rock back and forth. Kara jumped out just as Delia finished off her last man. However, the tower was already collapsing, and Kara's jump was too short. Luckily, Delia was able to grab hold of her sister's arm and with the help of Aurin, they were able to pull Kara back to safety.

As the tower collapsed, the men below began to run for the lives. Some of them were crushed beneath the falling debris while others broke ranks entirely. The center of Imbor's walls were secured. On the northern wall, the attack hadn't been as fierce. Despite the tower continuing to unload men, the Anayans and Khalians on that side were holding. Unfortunately, the same could not be said about the southern wall. The entire wall was being flooded by Numerans. Most of the defenders on that side were either dead or fighting a losing battle for their lives. Soon, the Numerans would push along the walls and inside the city itself. A decision had to be made quickly.

"Nema!" Kara called out.

"Yes, princess?" Nema acknowledged.

"Call a retreat to the northern wall. We can't hold them here."

Nema had seen the situation himself. Retreating to the northern wall meant they would be trapping themselves. However, it also meant they could consolidate their remaining defenses. There wasn't much of a choice at this point. Nema had also seen the girl take out a siege tower by herself so he was disinclined to argue with anything she suggested.

The sun had passed midday. Somehow, they had survived up to this point. However, the day was almost over, and everyone knew the end was soon near. The northern wall would be their last line of defense.

****

General Bellus watched in stunned fascination as the siege tower at the center of the walls collapsed. He felt no anger or panic. He couldn't even figure out how it happened. He saw a ballista bolt exit through the top ramp and assumed something about that last shot weakened the structure. He had to give the Anayans credit for the creativity as well as their incessant luck.

The battle itself was in no jeopardy. The southern wall was already being overwhelmed. Soon, Bellus would send the second wave of siege towers. In combination with the force that had already taken the southern portion, they would make quick work of the rest of these defenders. Before the sun set on this day, Imbor will have fallen and the Anayan campaign would come to an end.

****

The remaining defenders had to fight their way to the northern section of the wall. Kara didn't know how many defenders still remained but just looking around made it clear that the number was too small. The Numerans had already begun flooding into the city. Kara could hear screams coming from all around. These were not the screams of soldiers fighting and dying but of women and children.

The thought of the innocent being butchered angered Kara more than she'd ever felt in her life. Instead of continuing the retreat, she stopped and charged at the incoming enemy. She unleashed all the fury she had inside at these men, cutting them down, two or three at a time.

"Kara!" Aurin called out.

It had been bad enough when Kara had jumped into the siege tower earlier but now the girl seemed almost suicidal. Aurin entered the fray as well, trying to protect the princess. In truth, Kara was doing a fine job by herself. The advancing army was actually being held back by this lone woman.

"Kara, we need to get out of here." Aurin said as he grabbed her arm.

Aurin could see the fire in her eyes. It was the first time he'd seen such anger in her face and it made him uncomfortable. Even those times Kara would glare at him after he invaded her privacy didn't come anywhere near to this. However, the sight of Aurin seemed to calm the young woman. She nodded her head and proceeded to follow him.

Just then, they heard someone yelling from close by.

"Please! Help us!" they heard a woman scream.

There was an old woman carrying a small infant in her arms. Behind her was a company of Numerans chasing her. Once again, Kara's anger grew. It was bad enough that these bastards were killing the innocent but to send an entire company after one woman and a baby was cowardice. Kara moved forward and stood between the woman and the men coming after her. Aurin fought alongside the princess but this time, the force was too large for the two of them alone.

Kara was knocked down to the ground with Aurin unable to get to her. Kara closed her eyes and prepared herself for the killing blow when a spear flew through the air, killing the man standing over her. Kara looked back to see that Delia had returned with the rest of the surviving Khalians. There were only about twenty of them left but they moved forward to protect their future queen and her royal guard. Along with them, were several Anayans. They would not abandon the princess who had fought to defend them.

The attacking Numerans retreated for the time being. They weren't prepared to encounter this type of resistance so close to the end of the battle. This pause also gave the defenders time to assess themselves.

The northern gate was the only section of the entire city still held by the Anayans. The battle was over, and everyone knew it. Imbor had fallen and along with it, the entire Anayan nation. There were only one-hundred-fifty defenders remaining along with one ballista and one bolt. Kara looked around at the sullen faces around her and couldn't help but abandon hope herself. For the first time since she'd entered the city, Kara was tired. All she wanted was some rest before the end came.

Kara noticed the boy from earlier, the one with the missing arm. He'd somehow survived the second assault along with the retreat to the northern wall. She smiled to herself as she thought of the odds. She sat down on the ground next to the boy, giving him a warm friendly smile. He looked up at her and despite being wounded and close to death's door, returned her smile.

"What's your name?" Kara asked.

"I beg your pardon, Your Highness?" he asked, surprised that a woman of such high birth cared enough to ask.

"Your name. I never asked it."

"It's Vima, your highness."

"Kara. My name's Kara."

The boy was still obviously reluctant to use Kara's name. He'd always been taught to adhere to the formalities of society. Kara was a princess while he was only a blacksmith's son. Vima chuckled to himself, thinking about how silly it all was. They were surrounded by the enemy, on the cusp of death, and he was still holding onto a meaningless tradition that meant nothing in the end.

"Siege tower." Nema called out softly from the top of the wall.

It was clear by the tone of Nema's voice that the man was tired as well. His voice no longer carried the urgency nor authority of before. Now, it was a voice of acceptance for what was to come.

Kara climbed the steps to see the tower approaching. There was a single tower coming towards their position, but it wasn't the only one on the battlefield. More towers were approaching the other sections of the wall and Kara couldn't help but chuckle. It was pure overkill. The Numerans had already taken the rest of the city yet they were still sending more men. It was as if victory wasn't enough for the Numerans, they had to stomp the opposition into the dust.

Well then, let's go out with a bang. Kara thought.

In one last act of defiance, Kara aimed the final ballista herself. It had already been loaded with the bolt and all she had to do was hit the trigger on the side. Everyone's eyes were on Kara as she raised the hammer and slammed the trigger with all her might. The mechanism fired, the bolt soaring into the air. The bolt seared into the side of tower, right at the wheel. It was a one in a million shot. The two wheels of the siege tower fell off while the entire structure lost its balance and collapsed on its side. The men below ran for their lives and the entire left of the Numeran formation collapsed into chaos.

The Anayans defenders cheered as their last ballista bolt caused pain to the enemy. It was a futile act in the end but that mattered little to the conquered.

"Their lines on that side have collapsed. That buys you enough time to leave." Nema said.

Kara gave Nema a puzzled look before asking, "What are you talking about?"

"You're getting out of here." he answered.

"The hell I am!"

Nema grabbed Kara by the shoulders and said, "Listen to

me! You are the only resistance left against Gradus and his insanity. You must prepare your people. You must leave!"

"I am not going to abandon you!" Kara shouted back.

"If you do not leave, you are abandoning us all."

The words struck Kara harder than any blow she'd received all day. Nema wasn't wrong. Khalia was the last hope for any type of resistance against Numera. As much as it pained Kara, living to fight another day was the best way she could still serve the people – her own as well as the Anayans.

"You could come with us." Kara said.

"There are only enough horses to get you and your men out of here." Nema explained.

"The children. We could take some of the children."

"They will only slow you down. You have to be quick." Nema looked out into the battlefield once more. "Quickly! Before they can recover!"

Kara looked around to see that the Anayans had already prepared the horses for her. The Khalians themselves were prepared to carry out whatever order she gave. As Kara made her way to the steps that led down the walls, she wiped the tears from her face. She turned towards the people who now looked to the ground in defeat.

"People of Anaya, hear me!" Kara shouted as all eyes turned towards her. "There is nothing I can say right now to make things right. I'm leaving, you're staying. Most of you won't survive the day while I'll be at the royal palace in Khalia in a few days. It's not fair. I would trade anything to stay with you at this moment."

Kara wanted to stay strong, but she couldn't help the tears as they flowed down her face. She could barely look them in the eyes as she continued speaking.

"Some say that I'm a goddess but as you can see, I don't have any powers. I don't perform miracles and there's nothing remarkable about me. I am just like any one of you. You are a people of honor and courage. Upon my honor, I swear to you that I will return. Your time will come, and you will be liberated. I don't know how I'm going to do it or even where to begin but I promise you that if it's the last thing I do, I will not forget you and I will return for you. I swear this on my life, on my people, and everything I hold dear in this world!"

As Kara declared this promise she wanted to leave quickly. She couldn't look at the people she was abandoning. However, the people did not feel abandoned. For some strange reason, they felt hope. They felt as if they had heard the words of the divine. As Kara quickly climbed down the steps, she paused as every single Anayan kneeled before her. They believed the words she said. They believed she would remember them and return for them.

The other Khalians, including Delia and Aurin, were already on their horses waiting for Kara. As Kara got to her mount, it was Vima who held her hand and helped her up.

Vima handed Kara a small knife and said, "Here, princess. So that you will remember us."

Kara immediately got off her horse to give the boy a hug. She didn't want to let go. She didn't want to leave.

"Kara, please. You have to leave now." Vima calmly told her.

Kara got back on her horse and the Khalians rode out of the gate. The tears in her eyes made it almost impossible to see what was in front of her.

"It's funny, isn't it?" Delia asked.

"What is?" Aurin asked.

"Her entire life, Kara's been hated at home." Delia answered. "It was a bunch of strangers in a foreign country that treated her like family."

"Sounds like a fairytale." Aurin said.

"Well then, let's make sure it has a happy ending." Kara added.

****

Bellus had been furious when the siege tower on the left formation collapsed onto his men. The battle was all but over and suddenly, dozens of his men had been killed in an instant.

It wasn't even skill that had done the deed. It was a lucky shot from a ballista.

As Bellus struggled to coordinate with his captains to get the left side back in order, he saw the northern gate to the city open up. A handful of riders left the city and made for the break in the lines. It was already too late to issue any orders. The riders were going to escape.

The riders stampeded through the tangled mess that was the Numeran left. They met no resistance as they rode through. At the riders headed north, Bellus caught sight of the long red hair of two of them. It was the goddess and her sister.

"General, should we send riders to pursue them?" a captain asked.

Bellus considered it for a moment but decided against it. He still had a battle to finish. He'd already lost two siege towers and hundreds of men. He wasn't going to leave anything else to chance.

"Don't bother." Bellus responded. "The little girl runs away and abandons her allies inside. Now I know everything there is to know about this so-called goddess."

CHAPTER 4

Kara noticed how busy it was in the city as she and her two friends rode through the streets. Although busy, it was somehow eerily quiet. People were not saying much to each other. Everyone in the country knew what was waiting beyond the Yandu River. Refugees had been fleeing from Voya since it would be the first city to be attacked once the Numerans were done fording the river. It was expected that once Voya was sacked, refugees from Nabu would begin to arrive at Andor.

The influx of people had been a logistical nightmare for the council. Andor was simply running out of room to house everyone. On top of that, food was becoming scarce. The royal granary, which housed the emergency food supplies, were running low. With the additional refugees expected to come from Nabu, Khalia was in the midst of a major crisis before the invading army had even attacked.

Archbishop Tula suggested they close the gates at one of the council meetings. Kara scoffed at the idea. The man would abandon his own mother if it benefitted him. Luckily, she wasn't the only one appalled by this suggestion. The rest of the council unanimously agreed that they couldn't just abandon their own people. It was the only issue in which everyone was in agreement.

As they passed the church on the royal grounds, Kara grimaced and looked away. She wasn't opposed to the religion of her people. However, the beliefs of her people had haunted the young woman since before she was born. She couldn't help but feel some resentment towards the church. Especially when the church was being led by a snake called Tula.

The Goddess

Kara couldn't imagine how a man like Tula had ever become Archbishop. When the Archbishop dies, the bishops around the country would gather together to vote on a new one. This meant Tula had to be voted in by the spiritual leaders of the nation. Just how this occurred was unfathomable to Kara. Surely, she couldn't have been the first to see how big of an opportunist the man was. Kara's father had refused to answer any questions regarding the matter. Therefore, Kara knew it probably had something to do with her. She knew that Tula, who was a bishop at the time of her birth, was the first to suggest she be executed on the grounds that she was a curse to the Khalian people. Kara had a feeling the great majority of bishops either openly or secretly agreed with him which led to his election to the highest spiritual office in the nation.

There were still some good people at the church though. Reverend Miru was someone Kara had always confided in. He was going on fifty years and should've been a bishop by now at the very least. Instead, he was relegated to a reverend of a small church outside the city walls. Apparently, his friendship with Kara was the reason. The man claimed to have no regrets, but Kara felt sorry for him, nonetheless.

Kara still remembered the first time she met the man. Kara was thirteen at the time and was living in the city with Delia and Gillard. One day, she couldn't take the torment from the citizens anymore. Usually, Delia would always hold her and remind her of how much she was loved by the people that mattered. However, on that particular day, Kara was angry. She was angry at the church and this stupid religion that labeled her as a mistake. Kara had always been able to resist her father's offer to take her home but on this day, she had made up her mind to give up this futile crusade and return to the comfort of the palace. Kara ran away from the merchant's shop, out of the very city itself, and went into the church near the farms in order to curse at Yalka. As Kara stood at the altar and yelled all types of profanity at the god, the reverend had snuck in behind her.

At first, Kara felt as if it couldn't get any worse. Not only was she labeled as the "devil's child," there was now a man of the cloth who had witnessed her cursing the god's name.

Instead of reprimanding her, the reverend sarcastically said, "If you truly are the reincarnation of Yalka, you're just cussing yourself out."

Kara chuckled at the thought. The irony of it was pretty funny to her. The man sat her down and listened to her plights. She told him everything she'd been through and everything she ever wanted to say. For some reason, the man was so easy to talk to. Kara had associated church officials as being antagonistic towards her, but this man was different. Thus, began a long friendship between her and Reverend Miru.

Kara had continued to go back to the church at least once a week afterwards. She got to know the man and had many talks with him about various topics. Sometimes it would be about the prophecy and her own divinity. Other times, it could be as simple and pointless as which type of cheese was better suited towards dinner. In some ways, Reverend Miru knew her better than Aurin or even Delia.

Even after Kara returned to the royal palace, she continued to visit Reverend Miru. Whenever she went, no matter what he was in the middle of, he always made time for her. She found out that the reverend was one of the few church leaders to speak out against Tula's idea to execute Kara when she was born. He'd always defended the girl by arguing that they could not know the will of Yalka. Of course, Tula took the opposite approach and argued that he himself was the voice of Yalka in this world. This latter approach apparently worked better since Tula became Archbishop and Miru was left to rot in a small church in the middle of nowhere.

When Kara had first begun talking to Reverend Miru, she told him how much she hated the church and sometimes even the people of the city. Miru understood but also advised her to prevent her heart from filling with hatred.

"Do not hate them, Kara. Pity them. They are afraid, and because they are consumed by that fear, they try to make you less frightening to them." he told her.

"So, why do they have to take it out on me?" Kara asked.

"Because it is easier. They are always two choices. Either to hate and blame someone else for their problems or work to make themselves better. Guess which is easier."

"I guess the first."

"Exactly. You are better than them, Kara. You will not take the easy way."

This was why Kara decided to remain in the city despite her father offering to take her home each day. She knew it would be difficult, but in the end, she would become a better person for it. She also realized that hatred was a poison. If she let hatred consume her, she would become just like the people who treated her like filth. If it were not for Reverend Miru, Kara feared what she would've become.

Kara felt it a shame that not every church had a leader like Reverend Miru. Instead, most seemed to have a man like Tula. As much as she hated to say it, she felt the church would never be a true spiritual refuge as long as it was corrupted by men whose hearts were filled with fear and hatred.

The three riders entered the royal stables. For something called the "royal" stables, it was quite plain compared to other stables in the world. In fact, there were farmers with fancier stables than these. A boy sitting on a stool stood up as the three entered. He was a stable boy named Breka. He was an unimpressive boy of thirteen years. The other children made fun of him for two reasons. First, he was an orphan. His mother was a maid in the royal palace until she passed away when the boy was only seven. King Atlin refused to throw the boy onto the streets so he was put in charge of the stables. The child seemed to have an affinity with the horses and was a hard worker despite his age. The second reason for the incessant teasing was due to his size. For a boy of thirteen years, he was incredibly small. Even King Atlin felt the boy might have some type of disease. However, the doctors who examined him all said that there was nothing wrong with him. He was just delicate. General Gallus once told the king that he was concerned the boy might not be suited for the mandatory military service.

As Kara got off her horse, she smiled at the boy and asked, "What are you writing?"

Breka always kept a book with him. He wrote all manner of things from stories to poetry. When he wasn't at the stables, he could be found in the royal library.

"Just some poetry." Breka answered.

"Can I take a look?" Kara asked.

"It's... it's not ready yet." he stammered.

Kara had known Breka his entire life. She never thought the boy's size to be a problem. After all, Delia was not much bigger than the boy, but she was the most skilled warrior in the nation. If there was anything wrong with him, Kara felt it was his confidence. For years, Kara had asked the boy to show her his writings, but the boy always refused. He just never felt he was good enough.

Kara sighed and said, "Maybe later then."

"Yeah. Later. Have a good meeting, princess." he called out as she left.

"See you later, Breka." Delia said.

As the three walked out of the stables towards the royal palace, Delia turned to Kara and asked, "Has he ever shown you his writings?"

"Maybe he will one day." Kara answered.

"I stopped asking years ago." Aurin added.

The three friends stopped just short of the entrance. No one was looking forward to this meeting, but it was necessary. Bracing themselves for the inevitable, they pushed the doors to the royal palace open and entered the main throne room.

****

As the three friends entered the throne room, Kara was glad to see that they were early. She didn't want to start the day off by being on the receiving end of a stinging remark by one of the generals or Tula. After so many years of it, she had become accustomed to the way they treated her. However, she wasn't in a very good mood today and wanted to keep the number of verbal conflicts as low as possible. There would be enough of that when the meeting officially started.

King Atlin was already sitting on his throne. There was a large rectangular table set up with the king at the head. The generals would sit along the table, five to each side. Besides the king, there was General Gallus sitting on the left side of the table, closest to the king. Being the royal guard to King Atlin, he never left the king's side. Unlike other Khalians, General Gallus didn't have the characteristic red hair and pale skin of the people of the land. Gallus wasn't originally from Khalia. His mother was one of the few people allowed to immigrate into the reclusive country when Gallus was in his teens. It hadn't been easy for Gallus to grow up in a land where he was looked upon with suspicion for no other reason than his appearance. However, over time, he earned the respect of the people and no one questioned his character anymore.

There was also General Yusa sitting a seat apart from Gallus. Kara had always liked General Yusa. He was the only general other than Gallus who treated Kara with any respect. The man was never very religious, which was a point of contention with Tula. Tula seemed to like the generals he could control and influence. This was also the reason why Yusa never looked at Kara the same way most people did. He didn't care about the prophecy nor what the church said about the girl.

"General." Kara greeted Gallus as she passed by him.

"Princess." Gallus responded.

Gallus let out a heavy sigh. It had been years since the girl had called him "uncle." In fact, he remembered the first day she started calling him General. It was during her two years amongst the citizens when Kara was only thirteen. He had accompanied Atlin to go see Kara in Gillard's shop. As always, Atlin was trying to convince the girl to spare herself from the people's persecution and come back home. When Atlin walked away for the hundredth time, heartbroken to see his daughter suffer, Gallus finally decided to speak up.

"Kara, your father is just trying to do what he feels is best for you." Gallus told her.

The look Kara gave him was something Gallus would never forget. It was as if she were looking at a stranger. The little girl who ran into his arms whenever she got scared was no longer there. That girl had been replaced by something strong but cold at the same time.

"I think I know what's best in this situation, General." she replied.

Being called "General" by the girl he helped raise felt worse than any wound he'd ever suffered before. It felt like he had lost a daughter himself. He couldn't find the words to reply. After what felt like an eternity of silence, Gallus could only say, "As you wish, princess."

From that point on, the relationship between them was never the same. Kara was the princess and he was her father's royal guard. She was no longer the little girl who twirled around in her pretty dress. He was no longer the uncle who told her how beautiful she looked in it.

Gallus never said it out loud, but he longed for the days when he could call her Kara again. He longed to hear the intimate words identifying him as family, come from her lips. Now, he just resigned himself to sighing deeply each time she referred to him by the cold emotionless rank.

Kara and Delia took their seats next to their father, Kara on his right and Delia on his left. Aurin stood on the right side, near Kara. Atlin smiled as his daughters came shuffling in. He couldn't blame them for not wanting to be here. Half the time, even he didn't want to. The girls still managed to put a smile on his face. They were both smart, strong, and beautiful. Regardless of the fact that Delia wasn't of his own blood, she was still as dear to him as Kara was.

As Delia took her seat, Atlin looked at the young girl and smiled. He reached out and touched his daughter's hair as only a father who dotes on his daughter could. Delia on the other hand, frowned as her father did this. She loved her father, but she wished he wouldn't do this type of stuff with other's around. He still treated her like a child despite everything she'd seen and been through in the past few months.

Atlin just chucked to himself as he removed his hand. He looked over at Kara and saw that the girl was trying to keep her laughter hidden as she witnessed her sister's reaction to his touch. Teenagers were the same the world over. It didn't matter their gender, their experiences, or where they came from. Every single one of them wanted to grow up fast. They hated when their parents treated them like children. Of course, once they actually became adults, they would do anything to have their parents dote on them once again.

Atlin remembered how Kara was the same way. When she came back from her studies in Imbor at eighteen, he remembered doting on her day and night. Part of it was because he had missed her so much over the two-year span. The other part was because of how proud he was of her. Despite all the obstacles and hatred she had fallen victim to in her life, the girl had grown up to be exceptional. Atlin couldn't be prouder of the girl.

"How were the cliffs?" Atlin asked Kara.

Kara sighed at the mention of the peaceful spot and answered, "A bit windy today but nice."

"Maybe I'll go there with you next time."

Kara chuckled and said, "You haven't been out there since I was a child."

This was true. The last time he had been out there was eighteen years ago. It was the very day Yalka had blessed him with his second daughter, Delia.

When Kara was a child, Atlin would often take her out by the cliffs. Kara loved overlooking the scene from up high but Atlin preferred riding the horses along the beach below. It had been a warm summer day, at least as warm as Khalian whether could get. It was rare that you could dip your feet into the freezing cold waters of the Artic Sea as the waves lapped against the sand. Kara took full advantage of the situation and ran around barefoot along the shore. Every once in a while, the excited five-year-old would jump into the oncoming wave, getting her dress wet.

Atlin and Gallus rode their horses side-by-side slowly, talking about whatever came to their minds. It was a welcome time away from the city for all of them. Atlin and Gallus could speak of things other than royal business while Kara was away from all the animosity the people brought towards her. At this stage, Atlin had still sheltered Kara from the brunt of their hatred. Still, the little girl was smart enough to know that people didn't like her too much.

As Atlin and Gallus were arguing about who would win the annual horse races, Kara skipped off into the distance.

"Kara! Don't get too far ahead!" Atlin yelled after her.

"Let her have her fun." Gallus told him.

"Yeah, then she falls into the water and gets swept away by the current." Atlin said sarcastically.

"At least the priests wouldn't mind." Gallus joked.

Atlin glared at his friend as if to tell him his joke wasn't funny. At that moment, Kara ran up to them and started screaming, "Daddy! Uncle Gallus! There's a baby over there!"

At first, Atlin and Gallus just stared at each other wondering if the girl was just pretending or being serious. That was when they heard the soft sounds of a crying infant. Both men looked out into the distance to see a basket near the water.

"Come, Kara!" Atlin said as he grabbed the girl and swept her up onto his horse.

The two men spurred their mounts towards the basket as quickly as they could. The waves were rocking the basket and it looked the small wooden container would be swept into the water at any moment.

As the two men got to the basket, Atlin quickly dismounted and told Kara, "Stay on the horse."

Atlin grabbed the basket just as another wave came crashing into the shore. There was no telling how long the baby had been there. The water from the sea had soaked the blanket the infant was wrapped in. He took the baby out and coddled her into his arms. From the floral pattern on the blanket as well as the child's clothes, Atlin guessed it was a girl. Atlin looked around to see if anyone was around to claim the child.

"Do you think the child was abandoned?" Gallus asked.

"Looks like it." Atlin answered.

An emotion of pure unadulterated anger swept through Atlin. He couldn't believe how heartless people were. It was bad enough to kill a child but to leave the child to die a slow and painful death was indescribable. The mother or father probably left the basket near the shore hoping the waves would carry the girl off into the water. If Atlin ever found out who was responsible, he'd order their execution without a second thought. For now, he had to make sure the girl was alright.

Atlin took his cloak and wrapped the child in it. He removed the soaked blanket and clothes so the child wouldn't freeze to death. He had been right about the child's gender. Atlin put the blanket and clothes into the basket and handed the entire thing to Gallus. He thought of leaving the basket entirely, but the child might grow up wondering where she came from. It would be nice to have items for the girl to take a look at, should she wish.

Atlin handed the child to Kara and climbed back onto the horse. They began heading back to the city as the child began to cry.

"Keep her warm, Kara." Atlin told his daughter.

"I will, daddy." she answered.

Gallus couldn't help but wonder what the king intended to do with the child. The king could hand her over to be raised in the church. He could also just have the maids in the royal palace raise the girl.

"So, what do you plan to do with her?" Gallus asked.

Atlin didn't answer immediately. He began to wonder that himself. The baby had stopped crying and Kara was speaking to her softly.

"I've never had a sister before. Do you want to be my sister? I'll bet we'll be best friends forever." Kara whispered to the girl.

Both Atlin and Gallus heard Kara's words despite them being soft and low. Both men looked at each other as the question of what to do with the girl was answered for them.

Gallus rolled his eyes and said, "Great. Kara and now an orphan."

Gallus didn't go into details about that statement for Kara's sake but Atlin understood exactly what he meant. It was bad enough that Atlin was raising the "devil's child." Now, Atlin would be raising an orphan. The royal house would be seen as a circus to the people. Archbishop Tula would be given more ammunition to use against the reigning king. There was a chance Tula might even take the opportunity to declare the king "unfit" to rule. It wasn't likely that Tula would take it that far. Atlin was still loved by the people despite the complete opposite sentiment for his daughter. Still, the thought would go through Tula's head and that was always dangerous.

Atlin sighed at the inevitable quandary that awaited him. He looked down at the child who was now smiling as Kara played with her.

"What do think we should call her?" Atlin asked his daughter.

"Delia!' Kara immediately answered.

"Delia..." Atlin began.

Delia was a character in a Khalian legend. She was a mythical figure who went around the country defeating all manner of supernatural beings. Atlin wondered where his daughter had heard the legend. The story itself was not for the faint of heart. Not only were there terrifying scenes of violence but graphic descriptions of sexual acts. The version of the story in the royal library even had a scene where Delia makes love to a werewolf in order to cure him of the affliction.

Atlin heard Gallus chuckle at the mention of the name. He clearly didn't think the girl should've been exposed to the legend any more than Atlin did.

"Where did you hear that name?" Atlin asked Kara.

"Mara told it to me." Kara answered referring to the nursemaid in the palace.

"I'm going to have to have a talk with her." Atlin said to himself more than anyone else.

"I think Delia is a good name." Gallus said.

Atlin looked over at his friend wondering if he was being serious or not. The last thing Atlin wanted was for people to associate his new daughter with the plethora of sex acts the legendary character engages in during her adventures.

"It's strong, just like the girl. Besides, Delia is a national hero." Gallus added.

"Among other things." Atlin added as he glared at this friend.

Gallus saw the look Atlin had given him, but the man just waved the king's concerns away. Atlin sighed, realizing he'd been outvoted on the issue.

"Alright, Delia it is." Atlin relented.

"Yay!" Kara gleefully cried. "I can't wait to show you where we live. It'll be your home from now on too."

Atlin and Gallus smiled at each other as they saw how happy Kara was. She had always lacked for friends in the royal palace. The servants who brought their children didn't want them associating with the girl. The two men felt the presence of this new child would be good for the young princess. At the same time, the two men wondered what was in store for Delia as well.

****

King Atlin's memories were interrupted by the men filing into the room for the meeting. Each general sat in their assigned seats. They were seated according to the time in which they were promoted to the rank. The latest sitting furthest away from the king while the one's who had held the rank longest sat nearer. Although the men were technically the same rank, there was still an unspoken rule about being the elder. The men who held the rank the longest and sat nearer to the king, held much more influence and respect than the ones seated further away.

There was only one man besides Tula who was not a general at the table. This man was none other than Lieutenant Gidor, the same man who was once in competition against Aurin to graduate at the top of their class. Gidor had risen through the ranks faster than any other career soldier in Khalia's recent history. The man was exceptionally intelligent and always achieved high scores when it came to combat exercises. He was taking the place of General Hira, who was organizing and commanding the defenses in Voya. Gidor was considered Hira's right hand, and thus he represented the absent general in the meeting.

Everyone's eyes rolled as the last man entered the room. It was Archbishop Tula. He entered with the pomp of a man who knew the type of power he possessed. Despite agreeing with most of the generals in regards to their opinions about Kara, the man had a way of being incredibly disagreeable. He didn't care who he offended or made an enemy of. He truly believed that any enemy in his path would be crushed beneath his heel. No one understood where he got this arrogance from. It was no secret that the king himself didn't like the man. Perhaps he truly believed he was protected by Yalka and thought himself invincible. Whatever the reason, Tula feared no one, not even the wrath of the king.

Kara watched as Tula straightened out his golden robes and took a seat at the furthest corner of the table. Despite his seating arrangement, the man held more influence and power than anyone else except for the king. Kara wondered how her father had lasted his entire reign without ordering this man executed. It truly spoke to the character of her father that he allowed Tula to remain as powerful as he did. Technically, the king could order the execution of anyone for whatever reason. Obviously, neither Atlin nor any of the kings of the past ordered such things without cause. Ordering Tula killed would have brought the wrath of the church upon the royal house and labelled Atlin a tyrant in the eyes of the people. However, there were times Kara seriously thought the consequences worth it to be rid of Tula's poison on the land.

"Alright, everyone is here. Let's get this over with." Atlin announced.

Thirteen pairs of eyes, in addition to Aurin's, rolled. Everyone knew this meeting would be painful just like the last dozen times. The fact that the king acted as if this could be over quickly was cause for doubt.

"Give me a report on the defenses at Voya." Atlin ordered.

"It's going well, Your Highness." Gidor answered. "General Hira sent word about six days ago. Most of the citizens have evacuated. The rest should be ready to leave the city and be here within a few weeks. We have five divisions making up five hundred men already stationed within the city. Another three divisions from Nabu are on the march to reinforce them, ready to repel any attack."

Kara scoffed and said, "You realize there's an army of thousands across the Yandu."

"They have never met Khalian forces!" a general named Giltha screamed out in pride.

"Besides, what could a mere girl know about war." Tula added.

"That girl, is one of the only people in this room who has actually seen war." Gallus spoke out. "Show her some damn respect."

"Respect?!" Tula shouted as he stood up from his seat. "That girl is the reason we are in this mess!"

"Oh, I got to hear this." Delia said under her breath but loud enough that the few around her could hear.

"If she had not dragged a hundred of our best men into that hopeless situation in Imbor, we might have a better prepared army!" Tula continued. "Not to mention, her very existence is a crime against Yalka. Our god is punishing us for harboring this harlot!"

"Shut up and sit down!" Yusa told him. "No one wants to

hear about your religious babble."

"Religious babble it may be, but he speaks true when it comes to Imbor." another general by the name of Sulin chimed in.

"That's right. We all knew Imbor was a hopeless task, yet the princess decided to send our men to their deaths anyway." this time from General Farin.

Delia couldn't take it any longer and said, "Might I remind everyone that the men who went to Imbor all volunteered to be part of that division. Also, if I remember correctly, the Archbishop was a proponent of sending the Anayans said aid."

Tula's face visibly turned an angry red at being challenged by the teenage girl. At the same time, he couldn't argue against her logic.

"You shut your mouth, you dumb little girl!" Tula shouted back.

This time, Gallus stood up in anger and said, "Don't you dare talk to her that way!"

"I'll talk to her whichever way I please. I am the representative of Yalka in this council!" Tula shot back.

Yusa stood up this time and shouted, "Enough with your bullshit! You are the representative of the devil if I believed in such nonsense!"

"Blasphemy!" Tula cried.

By now, everyone was on their feet shouting profanities at each other. Aurin was the only one standing that hadn't said a word. The ones that were still seated were Atlin, Kara, Delia, and surprisingly, Gidor. The young man sat at the furthest end of the table, opposite Tula. His eyes rolled as he once again witnessed the council devolve into a circus. Gidor had been at the last six meetings and every single one of them turned out like this eventually. The time between the meeting's start and the arguments was actually getting shorter. As eager as he was to serve Khalia, he was getting sick of the politics himself. The man had trained to be a soldier, not a politician.

The Goddess

"Enough!" Atlin shouted.

It was rare for the king to raise his voice like this but when he did, the halls boomed at the deep authority it carried. Everyone immediately shut their mouths but remained standing as they eyed one another as if swords could be drawn at any minute. Delia actually wished swords would be drawn and the herd thinned. She felt the decision-making could go a lot more smoothly if some of these people were not here.

"If the members of this council cannot control themselves, perhaps we should recess and convene again at a later time." Atlin suggested.

The king's words were a welcome gift from this ceaseless quarrel. Some of the men just walked out without looking back. Others stood there waiting to be excused by the king. The king waved away those still in the room in frustration as he himself walked out towards his quarters.

As Kara, Delia, and Atlin were left in the room alone, Kara turned to Delia and said, "That went about as well I thought it would."

"Really? I thought it would be at least a half hour longer before they started going for each other's throats." Delia responded.

Kara sighed and rubbed her eyes. The recesses usually lasted from half an hour to an hour depending on the mood of the generals. King Atlin stopped trying to enforce discipline when it came to this. The generals were left to return when they felt like it. Just then, a boy ran into the throne room and handed an envelope to Kara.

"Message for you, princess." the boy said as he left just as fast.

Kara opened the envelope and took out the note. It read:
Kara, please come see me when you can. I have something urgent to speak to you about. – Reverend Miru.

In the ten years Kara had known the reverend, he had never asked Kara to come visit him. Kara would usually pick a day she wasn't too busy and just show up at the church. It was highly unusual and Kara hoped her friend was alright.

"What is it?" Delia asked.

"Reverend Miru wants to see me." Kara answered.

Kara got up and headed out the door, Aurin following close behind.

"You're going now?" Delia asked. "The council can reconvene at any minute."

Kara gave Delia a smile and said, "I'm sure they won't miss me."

"You want me to come with?"

"No, stay here. Father will need at least one of his daughters in attendance."

Delia slumped back into her chair.

Lucky. Delia thought to herself as her sister and Aurin left the room.

CHAPTER 5

Parin stood guard near the walls of Nabu as the sun shone down on his face. It was only midday and Parin would not be off duty for another couple of hours. He had only graduated from his four years of mandatory service two months ago. Usually, after graduation, the men would either choose to remain in Andor as career soldiers or return home to pursue other interests. Since Parin had been born and raised in Nabu, he decided to return home. However, instead of taking over his father's blacksmith, he was conscripted into the reserve force due to the Numeran threat on the horizon.

There were only about two hundred soldiers in Nabu at the moment, the great majority having marched to Voya in order to reinforce it. Parin felt that even these two divisions at Nabu were unnecessary. Everyone knew the Numerans were fording the river and Voya would be hit first. This was also why the great majority of citizens were still in the city. They were getting ready to evacuate to Andor but for now they could take their time. Word from Voya would come quickly once the Numerans crossed the river. Only then would the people begin the trek to the capital.

Unlike Andor and Voya, Nabu did not have stone walls. The city was surrounded by wooden palisades to keep out the wildlife. Since Nabu was protected by the Karisian Mountains to the south, the people never felt threatened by an outside force. Voya was always the first line of defense against any incursions. Either way, Khalia had never been attacked. Its only other bordering neighbor was Anaya and the Khalians had always had a friendly relationship with them. There were legends that Khalia and Anaya were at war in the past. However, since no official records of those times existed, most Khalians felt it was just that – legends.

This was why Parin and his fellow soldiers stood outside Nabu's walls, bored out of their minds. They knew nothing was going to happen. Even standing there on guard felt like a waste of time to most of them.

Parin shivered in his armor as a cold wind swept across the land. Despite the sun shining bright, it was still the middle of winter. Khalia was always cold but the winters were especially harsh. Even on a sunny day like today, the temperatures were freezing. There were many times Parin went back inside after a long day's duty to find his toes red and raw from the cold. It would sometimes take all night, sitting with his feet by the fire, in order to gain feeling in his appendages again.

Luckily, Parin only had to stand on guard three times a week. The only men required to be on duty were the ones assigned to guard the gate. Therefore, even though Nabu technically had two hundred soldiers in Nabu, only about fifty of them were ready to fight at a moment's notice. All fifty of them were on guard, surrounding the walls. Parin felt envious at the thought of the others who were inside and warm.

Parin let out a deep sigh and watched his breath freeze in the cold air. Just as he wondered how much longer he would have to be out here, he felt the ground move. He thought it was his imagination at first but when he looked at his companion standing next to him, he realized his friend had felt it too. He took a closer look at the ground and realized it wasn't just in his mind. The small stones on the ground were rattling as if thunder were clapping through the air during a harsh storm.

"What the hell is that?" Parin asked his friend.

"Earthquake?" his friend said.

Great. Parin thought. *The last thing we need is a quake.*

Earthquakes were rare in Khalia, but they did happen. They usually only lasted a few seconds but sometimes they would knock over branches and cause damage to the buildings.

The Goddess

However, this quake was not slowing down. It started to get louder, and the rumbling of the ground was getting more pronounced. The priests in the church always said Yalka was mad at the people of Khalia for sheltering the "devil's child." For an instance, Parin thought they might be right. This quake might be Yalka's vengeance on the people of the land.

Just then the alarm bell started ringing. As one bell rang, several others began to ring across the city. The bells were of a particular make and created a deep distinct sound. It was a sound Nabu had never heard before, yet everyone knew what it meant. It was a warning that they were being attacked.

Parin and his friend stared at each other in shock. They didn't know what to do. They couldn't even believe what the bells were indicating. What the hell happened in Voya? How come they didn't send any runners to warn them if the city had been taken? It didn't matter at the moment. If there was an attack, it would come from the east side.

As Parin and his friend began to run for the east wall, he saw other soldiers doing the same. They had come to the same conclusion as Parin and were making their way towards the most likely place of an attack. Just then, a soldier came running towards them.

"South gate! The captain orders everyone to the south gate!" the soldier shouted.

The soldiers immediately stopped in bewilderment. How could there be an attack on the south gate? Either way, everyone switched directions and began heading there. This was no time to think. It was time to defend their homes.

As Parin and the others got closer to the southern section of the wall, they could hear the unmistakable sounds of fighting. Screaming, shouting, and the clear ring of metal against metal began to pound against Parin's eardrums.

It couldn't be. Parin thought. *The Numerans couldn't have crossed the Karisians.*

Khalia's own scouts had never managed to find a path across the Karisians for centuries. It was deemed an impassable mountain range. Yet, the Numerans had somehow found a way in the dead of winter. Now, they were at literally at the doorstep of Nabu.

Parin's heart faltered as he reached the gate and saw the image before him. It wasn't just a small group attacking them. It was a massive army crowding to get through the gate. Parin couldn't tell how many there were. It was like a sea of black water rushing to flood the city. Parin wasn't the only one who stopped in his tracks as the massive wave rushed in and swarmed over anyone and anything in its way.

Parin finally saw one up close. A man whose eyes were full of murder charged at him screaming. The man raised his sword high and struck downward. Parin was only able to get his own sword up quick enough to block the killing blow. Still, Parin fell to ground, losing his sword in the process. As he crawled to escape the killing zone, someone grabbed his shield and flipped him over onto his back. He looked up to see another man, sword raised above his head, ready to strike down. Parin instinctively put his hands up to guard himself and closed his eyes awaiting the inevitable.

However, the blow never came. Several seconds went by, Parin frozen in place. When he gained the courage to open his eyes again, he saw the same man slump onto the ground next to him. Parin stared at the lifeless eyes of the man, cold and unblinking. Just moments ago, the same man was alive, ready to take Parin's life. Parin didn't know what happened and didn't care. He just wanted to get out of there. He stood up and ran, not bothering to look behind him.

All around Parin, Khalians were fleeing, some were soldiers in armor and others were civilians. Men, women, and children, all fleeing to get away from the deadly black fog coming to engulf them. Parin finally gained the courage to look back, to see how far ahead of death he was. Luckily the swarm had slowed down. The thing that slowed them down were the civilians, the ones who weren't fast enough or were caught by surprise. The Numerans were stopping to kill everyone. Some were tearing at the clothes of the women, ready to defile them on the spot. Parin continued to run as fast as he could while witnessing this horror.

Just then, Parin crashed into something, knocking him back down onto the ground. It felt like he had run into a wall.

"On your feet, boy!" the figure over him screamed.

It was Captain Tiva. Parin had crashed into the gigantic man and the captain hadn't even flinched. As the captain helped Parin to his feet, he nearly tossed the confused boy onto the top of a horse.

"You get to Andor! You tell them what's going on!" Tiva told him.

Parin didn't answer. His mind was still trying to put everything into place.

Tiva grabbed the boy by the collar and screamed, "Do you understand me, boy?"

"Yes... Yes, Captain!" Parin answered, finally coming to his senses.

"Go! Ride!" Tiva screamed as he slapped the horse's rear.

The horse flew off with Parin riding on top of it. Parin rode straight for the gate, passing by everyone screaming and hollering in fright. He felt sorry for leaving them. He was leaving them to die. However, he also knew he had a job to do. He had to get to Andor. He had to let them know. The fording of the river didn't matter. Voya didn't matter. The invasion had already begun and the city of Nabu was its first casualty.

****

Kara entered the dark church, taking in the sounds of the solitary building. It was so empty that something as small as a pin drop would echo against the walls many times over. Aurin stood by the door as he always did. Maybe it was because he wanted to give Kara her space, but the man never stepped deeper into the building for some reason. In fact, Kara had never seen Aurin enter a church. It was unusual because she had often seen Aurin praying. She wondered if Aurin worshipped another god besides Yalka. It would be scandalous for the royal guard to the princess to worship a foreign deity. If that were in fact the truth, and if it ever came out, Kara felt like the people would somehow blame it on her. The church most definitely would.

"Reverend?" she called out to no answer.

Kara went to the front of the altar. She took a knee and bowed her head. It wasn't that she was particularly religious. Besides, according to prophecy, she was in fact Yalka. However, just in case she wasn't, and the god did in fact exist, it probably wouldn't be too wise to offend him in his own sanctuary. Either way, it was always a nice sentiment to respect the customs of the people of the land. Even if the religion of the people saw you as an abomination.

"I always wondered why you did that." a voice from the foyer said. "After all, aren't you Yalka?"

Kara looked to the side and saw her dear friend Reverend Miru. The reverend stepped into the room and gave Kara a hug.

"How are you doing, dear girl?" Miru asked.

"Alright, given the circumstances." Kara answered.

Miru chuckled and said, "I can imagine."

"Are you alright? Your message sounded urgent." Kara asked with concern in her voice.

"Oh, I apologize for concerning you. It is urgent but nothing immediately life threatening."

As the two sat down on the pews in front of them, Kara jumped at the squeak it made as it echoed through the church. For some reason, Kara could never get over that loud sound. The first time she had come into this church, Kara was so startled by the sound she almost forgot why she was there in the first place. She couldn't believe nobody had repaired it in all these years. It went to show just how the other church leaders felt about Reverend Miru. In another church, if someone reported a broken candle, it would be replaced within minutes. In Miru's church, if the pews squeaked, the doors were unhinged, the roof caved in, they would just leave it for the good old blasphemous reverend to handle.

"How much do you know about the legend of Isa?" Miru began.

"I know the story but it's just that, a story" Kara answered.

Isa was a king during the early days of Khalia. His reign would've been uneventful had he not made certain claims in his diary. Isa was a great explorer in his younger days. He claimed to have found a mysterious door to Yalka's sanctuary during an exploration of the Arctic Sea. Nobody took his claims seriously, including the church.

"I want you to take a look at this." Miru said.

Miru searched through his bag and produced several pieces of paper and a role of parchment. As Kara skimmed through the papers, her eyes grew wide.

"Is this real?" Kara asked.

"I found it in this church's archives. I've been going through them for years, trying to organize them." Miru responded.

From the little that Kara had read, they appeared to be the lost pages of Isa's diary. The original diary was kept in the library of the royal palace. There were several pages missing, evidently having been ripped out. No one knew why or what was in them.

"This is a great historical find but is this really necessary at a time like this?" Kara asked.

Kara understood the importance of history and preserving records. However, the nation was facing a crisis. While the reverend was playing scholar, the nation was on the verge of annihilation. In a few days, Khalia may cease to exist altogether.

"Still jumping without looking." Miru teased as he poked Kara in the nose.

Miru had repeated this phrase countless times to Kara, usually when she jumped into things that got her into trouble. He'd been saying it to her since she'd been a child. He always treated her like one by poking her nose with his finger every time. In a way, Kara appreciated these moments. It reminded her that she still had much to learn and to keep herself from being rash.

Miru continued, "These pages go into detail about the supposed door to Yalka's sanctuary. He tells of a great power inside that could make an army unstoppable."

Kara raised her eyebrows at this mention. If Khalia could somehow get their hands on this power, they could potentially repel any attack Numera threw at them.

Miru chuckled and said, "Thought that might interest you."

"There's only one problem, no one knows where the sanctuary is." Kara said.

Miru sighed and said, "What did I say two minutes ago about jumping without looking?"

Kara rolled her eyes and stuck her tongue out, but she knew Miru was right. At the same time, she enjoyed acting like a child in front of Miru. It was the only time she could. She always had to put on a brave face and act like a leader for everyone else. Miru had seen Kara at her worst. He was the only one she could be immature and vulnerable with.

Miru took the rolled-up parchment and lightly tapped Kara's head with it.

"Here." he said.

Once again, Kara's eyes widened. It was a map to the sanctuary. It didn't just show the direction, it showed the exact location. It was located on an island, three days journey north of Andor. The map even went into detail about the island itself, identifying specific landmarks as well as a hidden entrance.

"A little too detailed to be fantasy, I think." Miru said.

"What do you want me to do? Drop everything and go after this thing?" Kara asked.

Miru stood up and said, "I don't *want* you to do anything. I gave you information. Please feel free to do with it as you will, princess."

Kara quickly gathered up everything Miru had handed her. She gave Miru a hug and said, "You can't stay out here. You have to evacuate inside the city."

Miru laughed and said, "I don't think I'll be welcomed with open arms."

"You will at the palace."

Miru thought about it and said, "Very well. I'll gather my things and head there as soon as I can."

As Kara headed for the exit, she looked back and said, "Don't take too long. Thank you, Reverend."

Kara and Aurin began heading back to the city with haste. The recess for the council was most likely over by now and they'd be late. Kara felt a bit torn about what Miru had shown her. Was she really thinking about leaving Khalia in its time of need to follow a legend? At the same time, Kara knew Khalia didn't stand a chance by conventional means. Numera was too powerful, both technologically and numerically. They needed some sort of advantage in order to overcome this trial.

Aurin had heard everything, being in the same room as them. He also saw the look on Kara's face and knew what she was thinking. If he were presented with the same predicament, he would be wracking his brain trying to decide what to do.

"So?" Aurin asked.

"So, what?" Kara responded.

"I was in the same room with you. You don't think I was listening?"

Kara sighed and said, "I don't know. What do you think?"

Aurin chuckled and said, "I think the old man has finally lost his mind."

Kara hesitated before asking, "What if it's true?"

"It's crazy. Either way. It's crazy to go after this thing, especially right now. It's crazy if it's real."

"Well, you can always stay here."

Aurin didn't say anything. Kara and Aurin both looked at each other with a smile. That last statement wasn't even funny. Wherever Kara went, Aurin went. That was the way their relationship worked. To hell and back with the both of them.

****

"General, what is taking so damn long?"

Bellus flinched at the Emperor's bellowing voice. It was only the first battle of the Anayan campaign and Bellus had already lost a third of his men. The Anayans were reputed to have the best archers in the world and that reputation was well-earned. Time and again, the Anayans fired their bows with pinpoint accuracy. Bellus was familiar with the phrase that every Anayan arrow fired would hit a target. It wasn't an exaggeration. Hundreds of arrows had been fired already. As Bellus examined the battlefield, he noticed that the only arrows on the ground were ones that had broken off inside his men or on their armor.

"Your Majesty, the Anayans control the high ground. I recommend we pull back and lay siege to the fortress." Bellus said.

"Nonsense! You have been at this all day! They must be running out of arrows!" Gradus said.

"Your Majesty, if we lay siege to the fortress they will eventually capitulate. No more men need to die." Bellus argued.

"They are soldiers! They are meant to die! Send in more soldiers until the Anayans run out of arrows!"

Bellus didn't know what else to do. The Emperor was insistent upon this bloody course. Bellus looked to his lieutenant who was holding the horn used to sound orders. The man looked at Bellus almost pleadingly. It was as if he was begging his general to reason with the Emperor. The truth was, Bellus felt the same way. He wanted someone else to give the order. He wanted someone to speak out against this dastardly order.

"I am done waiting, General!" Gradus shouted as he stood up.

That was all the encouragement Bellus needed. The next order out of the Emperor's mouth would be for his head. Then, the order to proceed forward would go on regardless. Bellus just looked towards his lieutenant and nodded. The horn sounded for one company to march forward.

Two-hundred men wailed at the sound of their doom.

The Goddess

None of them marched forward until the captains began to physically push the men. Eventually, the reluctant company began to move.

As the men came into the range of the Anayan archers, Bellus was surprised to find that the company hadn't been fired upon. Perhaps the Anayans had already run out of arrows. Perhaps no one had to die.

This changed when the Anayan horn sounded. The Anayans were just waiting for their enemies to get closer. A flood of arrows came raining out of the sky, slamming into the formation of men. The Numerans raised their shields but it was to no avail. The Anayans aimed at the feet of the men. When the men dropped their shields to protect their legs, the Anayans would finish them off with a shot to the head or body. Those who tried to run away only made for easier targets. They were shot in the back before they could even take a few steps. Soon, the entire company lay dead or dying on the ground, the entire area around them pooling in blood.

"Send a second company!" Gradus ordered.

Bellus couldn't believe what he had just heard. Hadn't the man seen enough? With his eyes closed, he nodded towards the lieutenant. Bellus couldn't bear to look the man in the eyes.

Once again, Bellus heard the horn sound and the next company wailing in despair. Bellus kept his eyes closed, as he heard the screaming and metal tearing as the arrows punched through armor and flesh.

"There! Now kill them all!" Gradus bellowed.

Bellus finally opened his eyes to see that some of his men had made it to the walls. There were only four of them. Nearly four-hundred men had been slaughtered within minutes for nothing. All they had to do was wait. If they had just waited, the Anayans would have surrendered.

With a nod towards his lieutenant, Bellus ordered the rest of the men forward. This would be a moment Bellus could never forget, even if he wanted to.

****

    Bellus awoke suddenly, cold from the sweat pouring from his body. It had been the same dream he had almost every night since it happened. It was day Bellus realized what kind of a man Emperor Gradus was. He was ruthless, impatient, and cared nothing for the men under his command. There had been many times Bellus wondered why he fought in this army. Whenever this question invaded his mind, he had to remind himself of the answer. He fought for his country. He fought because he cared about his men. If he left, Gradus might replace him with someone like Decimus. He fought because if he didn't, Gradus would have him killed.

    Bellus didn't fear death. He'd faced it many times before and accepted that he was a man of war who could die on the battlefield at any given moment. What Bellus feared was the Emperor's wrath. Bellus had heard stories of the tortures Gradus applied to his enemies as well as anyone who so much as displeased him. Bellus had seen much of this firsthand. He didn't want to end up like these people and so he continued to serve.

    "Are you alright, master?"

    Bellus looked to his left and saw the girl next to him. She was the same one he'd saved a few days ago from being part of the Emperor's throne bearers. He had learned her name was Nola. She wasn't part of the Battle of Imbor like Bellus had first suspected. She had been captured on a farm a few months before the battle. Her father was killed, her mother raped then killed, and Nola was taken to be a plaything for the men in the camp.

    She had grown so accustomed to her treatment by the men that she kept calling Bellus master, even though he repeatedly asked her not to. She was also shocked at how well she had been treated by him. Just giving her a share of his food was enough to put a smile on the girl's face. Apparently, she had been surviving off scraps the men had thrown at her like a dog for the past few months. It had been enough to keep her alive and put some flesh on her bones to keep her attractive but nothing like what Bellus offered.

She was also shocked that Bellus did not want to "use" her. She had immediately disrobed the first time when Bellus crawled into his bed for the night. He actually had to yell at her to put her clothes back on. Bellus immediately apologized to her for raising his voice but the girl was still confused and shocked. She couldn't understand why he kept her around if not for the entertainment.

Bellus didn't really understand it either. He had never seen slaves as more than tools to be used. Now, he was sharing his food, his tent, his bed, and even apologizing to one. It didn't just stop at sharing one's accommodations. Despite her referring to him by "master," she was quite a good conversationalist. Bellus hadn't realized how lonely he'd been until he began talking to the girl and getting to know her. He would have preferred if she were a man but just having a friend was something to look forward to at the end of a long day.

Friend? he thought to himself and chuckled.

Bellus never thought he'd ever call a slave a friend. However, that was the best word he could describe her as.

"Is there anything I can do for you, master?" she asked.

"Yeah. Stop calling me that." Bellus replied.

It was a hopeless request. The girl had been so conditioned to call people master over the past couple of months that she couldn't quit the habit. She also couldn't seem to see herself as anything more than an object. One time, Bellus and Nola were having dinner, talking and laughing about old times. The girl seemed to be breaking out of her slave conditioning. When she knocked over a glass of wine and spilled it on the floor, she immediately kneeled on the ground and offered to, "Do anything to make you happy, master."

It broke Bellus' heart to see her like this. He had come to care about the girl, and he worried for her. She was going to have a child soon. How was she supposed to be a proper mother if she saw herself as less than human? Would she pass that on to her own child? Bellus had seen generations of slaves back in Numera. Each parent passed on their servile attitude to the next generation. He didn't want Nola and her eventual family to end up like this.

"What time is it?" Bellus asked.

"It's evening. The sunset was only an hour ago." Nola answered.

Bellus had been so tired all day that he had decided to lay his head down a bit. He regretted that decision now. His revisit to the nightmare in his past as well as the fact that he woke up with a headache told him he should've stayed awake. As he got his armor back on, his headache intensified as a sudden cheering in the camp arose. Gritting his teeth, he exited the tent to see what the commotion was about.

"What the hell is going on?" he asked.

A captain went up to Bellus and saluted.

"Good news, General." the captain began. "The fording of the river has been completed."

"Excellent!" Bellus said with a smile.

His headache wasn't half as bad now. The army could finally move against Khalia. The waiting was over, and the Emperor would be happy.

The captain continued, "More good news, General. We received word earlier that Nabu to the west has fallen."

Bellus closed his eyes as his headache returned with force. It was good news for Numera that Nabu had fallen. However, it was bad for Bellus. Knowing Decimus, the man was probably already moving towards Andor. The bloodthirsty idiot would probably charge the walls of Andor with the three thousand men he commanded. Bellus had to act fast before Decimus got all those men killed. This meant crossing the river, taking Voya, and beating Decimus to Andor before he could do something foolish.

"Battle formations, captain. Get it done, and quickly." Bellus ordered.

"Yes, General!" the captain shouted before running off.

The Khalian campaign had already begun. Decimus had

struck the first blow. The end was near and Bellus could feel it.

****

King Atlin returned to the war council only to find that most of the generals were still absent. Besides Gallus, who entered with the king, only Yusa and one other general were back in the room.

Damn children! Atlin thought.

As Atlin took his seat on the throne, he noticed Kara was also missing. Delia was slumped in her chair, pouting and looking bored. Atlin had to laugh at the sight. As great of a warrior as she was, Delia was still a child and images such as this served to remind him of that.

"Where's your sister?" Atlin asked the girl.

Delia just shrugged her shoulders.

"You don't know? I find that hard to believe." Atlin said.

"I'm not my sister's keeper, father." Delia insisted.

Ugh! Teenagers! They're all the same the world around. Atlin thought.

Soon, all the men began returning one by one. Everyone was present except for Kara. No one seemed to say anything about the princess' absence. Most were probably glad she wasn't in attendance at all.

As the hours went by, there was more arguing, and nothing had been accomplished. If anyone thought Kara was the problem, this was proof that she wasn't. In fact, the arguments against her went on and on, longer than usual since the girl wasn't there to defend herself. Atlin, Delia, Gallus, and Yusa defended Kara whenever they could but it was a hopeless cause. These men had already made up their minds about her. To them, Kara's absence only proved she didn't care about the concerns of the nation.

Eventually, Kara returned from her little excursion with Aurin in tow.

Tula looked up and said, "Ah, the princess joins us now. The concerns of the nation obviously don't interest you!"

Kara ignored him and before she had even taken her seat, blurted out, "I need a ship."

Almost immediately, Kara's supporters raised their hands to their face and covered their eyes as if to say, "What is wrong with you?"

It was bad enough she wasn't liked by most of the council but now she was making outlandish demands during a time of crisis. Even Aurin stopped in the middle of the room, closed his eyes, and grimaced at the way Kara went about her request. It wasn't a request. In fact, it was a demand. As Kara took her seat, Aurin quickly made his way beside her where he could see the rest of the council. Everyone seemed to be at a loss for words. Tula himself didn't even know what to say. Kara might as well as have entered a church in front of the entire nation and announced that she was in fact the devil.

Tula finally got his senses back and asked, "Have you lost your mind?"

"I have it on good authority that there is a weapon that could help Khalia." Kara explained.

"Please, do share. What is this weapon?" Tula asked.

"Something that will help Khalia repel the Numerans." Kara said.

"Just where did you get this information?" General Sulin asked.

"From a confidential source." Kara answered.

Atlin sat next to his daughter thinking it couldn't get any worse. He considered reaching out and taking her hand just to shut her up. Atlin thought it was his lucky day when the front doors to the royal palace opened up and the council was interrupted by a young soldier.

The young soldier was Parin, bloody and exhausted but still alive.

"My Lord! Nabu has fallen!" Parin announced.

The entire room erupted at the news. Everyone was on their feet including the king and his daughters.

"What? Impossible!" General Farin shouted.

"How could they have taken Nabu without taking Voya first?" Gallus asked.

"The Numerans crossed the Karisian Mountains! They attacked from the south!" Parin explained.

There were more shouts of disbelief from the council. It shouldn't have been possible. The Karisian Mountains had never been crossed. The fact that Numera had done so with an army in the middle of winter didn't seem believable. Yet, the soldier in front of them was covered in blood and dirt. He had clearly been in battle.

"Silence!" the king shouted.

The panicked room immediately calmed down, waiting for their king to issue orders. All politics had gone out the window. The invasion had begun, and in the most unlikely way possible. They needed to decide what to do quickly.

The king began, "General Yusa, take your men towards Nabu. You will provide cover for anyone escaping from the city and slow down the advancing force. The fording of the river will not be far behind. Send word to General Hira in Voya to prepare for an attack. The rest of us will stay here to calm the citizens and prepare our city for the coming assault."

Looking around the room, Atlin could see the fear in everyone's eyes. Everything seemed so real now. Even with the Numerans on their doorstep, the war had seemed so far away. Now that the enemy had crossed the threshold and into their country, the reality was setting in.

"Get on it!' Atlin ordered.

Everyone left the room without argument, including the king. The time for arguing was over. It was time for action. Kara just hoped the action wasn't coming too late.

General Yusa stayed behind and motioned for Kara to come over. Delia and Aurin waited for their friend to finish speaking with the general.

"There's a ship in the south, just outside the city gates. The Arita." Yusa told Kara.

The Arita was a small experimental ship. It was named

after Kara's mother, the deceased queen and wife of King Atlin. The ship itself was intended to be used as a fast-moving supply ship. Construction on it began when Anaya was attacked. The idea was to use the ship to supply Anaya by sea. However, there were two problems. The Numeran navy had blockaded all of Anaya's docks and the Arita was so small, it couldn't carry enough meaningful supplies. The ship was permanently docked and intended to be used for scrap wood.

"Is it operational?" Kara asked.

"It is. You'll have to find your own crew, but the ship is small. Only about twenty men should suffice. Get your weapon. Quickly!"

"Thank you, General." Kara said as the man nodded and left.

Delia and Aurin walked up to Kara. Despite giving them their privacy, both of them had heard the entire conversation between Yusa and Kara.

"So, what's this weapon?" Delia asked.

Kara smiled at her sister and said, "Something that will help us."

Delia's faced dropped in disbelief as she said, "You don't know, do you?"

"Go pack your stuff. We leave in an hour. Aurin, get our men ready. We'll meet you at the dock." Kara ordered.

"Wait, you want me to leave you alone?" Aurin asked.

It would be the first time in five years the girl wouldn't be in eye sight of the man. However, this was urgent. The nation had never faced anything like this before and their mission might not only decide the fate of Khalia but the entire world.

Kara patted Aurin on the chest and said, "You're a big boy. You'll be fine."

The two girls left for their rooms leaving Aurin alone. He had to restrain himself from going after the princess, but he was given a job to do. He had to go find a crew and he knew just who to get.

CHAPTER 6

Kara was in her room rushing to pack as quickly as she could. She and Delia had to be out of there before their father caught on to what they were doing. Kara didn't even look at what she was putting into her bag. A lot of her clothes were lying all over her room. She cursed herself for not ever being able to keep it clean. It was one of her huge flaws. Her room would be clean in the morning and by the afternoon, it'd look like a hurricane had hit it. The servants used to clean her room but even they gave up after a while. It was fine by her. She liked living in a mess. Unfortunately, it was now coming to bite her in the ass.

Kara grabbed at whatever stuff was lying around. She'd pack now and worry about what to wear later. She only needed enough for the journey. As Kara was digging under her bed, her hand grabbed at something unusual. She pulled it out and realized what it was. It was the double-bladed staff she had invented.

The staff was the first time she'd experienced failure in front of the council. Shortly after Kara had returned from her studies in Imbor with Master Grishom, she realized how useless the first two years of the military training in Khalia really was. Since the men were only allowed to use a wooden staff in the beginning, Kara thought it'd be smart to attach blades on them. This way, they could be trained in traditional Khalian martial arts while at the same time learning to implement bladed weapons.

For two years, Kara had trained with the weapon she had invented. She developed new techniques rooted in Khalian martial arts. When she was confident she had something special, she presented it to the council only to be laughed out of the room. Kara went to her room, threw the staff on the ground and forgot about it until now.

It took another few council meetings and proposals to realize the staff wasn't the problem. The problem was the council and their attitude towards Kara. Whatever she proposed was shot down no matter how practical it was. Everything from her proposal to create a Khalian archery division to her suggestion that Khalia study Numeran steel technology were shot down. The proposal to study steel was actually rejected by Archbishop Tula on religious grounds. His exact words were, "We will use the technology Yalka provided for us, not the technology of the godless heathens."

Kara couldn't believe the ignorance. It was as if Tula believed Yalka developed iron or bronze technology. They were all developed by blacksmiths. Iron technology only came to Khalia after it was introduced through trade with Anaya. Surprisingly, most of the generals supported her idea. However, once Tula threatened to use the church to spread the word that the council was considering the use of the "devil's technology," the generals shut up and forgot about it.

"Just where do you think you're going, young lady?"

Kara turned around and dropped the staff at the sudden shock. Her father was standing in the doorway looking at her as she held a bag full of clothing. It was clear she was packing to go somewhere. Every excuse she could think of was running through her mind. She could say she was cleaning her room, but she'd never done that in her life. It was unlikely her father would believe she decided to do so right before the nation got invaded. She could also say she was running away because she was afraid but once again her father knew her better than that. So instead of coming up with an excuse, she just stood there, frozen with her mouth gaping open.

Atlin entered the room and picked the staff up off the floor. He twirled it around and examined the blades on either end of it.

"Still sharp." he remarked.

Atlin handed the staff back to Kara. He then grabbed a jacket and placed it around her. His hands rested on her shoulders as he looked at his strong, brave, and willful daughter.

"Pack warm. It'll be cold on the water." he said.

Kara's face changed from one of surprise to confusion. She thought her father would most certainly stop her from leaving.

"Wait, what?" she asked.

Atlin sighed and said, "Would I be able to stop you anyway?"

It was less of a question and more of a comment. From the day Kara was old enough to walk, the girl had a mind of her own. Whenever Kara said she would do something, she would do it. It didn't matter who or what was in her way. After a while, Atlin realized how strong the girl's will was and just accepted it as part of her charm.

"You're not going to stop me?" Kara asked.

Atlin laughed and replied, "As if I could."

Atlin sat the girl down on the bed and took a seat beside her. He held Kara's hand, knowing this could be the last time he'd see her. The Numerans could attack Andor before Kara returned from her journey. In a way, he was actually glad his daughter was leaving. Despite going into the unknown, it would also keep her away from the fighting.

"I remember when you were four years old." Atlin began. "I took you down to the Yandu river and there was a tree by the water. You climbed the tree and said you were going to jump off the branch and into the water. Of course, me and your uncle Gallus were frantic, trying to get you down from there."

Kara smiled at the memory. Even though she was young, she still remembered it well. The truth was, she was scared to jump from that high. Something in her had told her to push herself, to overcome that fear though.

Atlin continued, "Your uncle Gallus was pleading for you

to come down and I was threatening to punish you if you jumped. Still, you did it. Now, besides being an unruly child, I realized then, that no matter how hard it may be for you or what I say, you were going to do what you wanted. When you did your two years with Gillard, that only reinforced everything."

"I almost gave up when I was with Gillard." Kara admitted.

"Almost being the key word." Atlin added with a smile. "As a father, I just had to make sure that you learned right from wrong. That what you wanted to do, was the right thing."

"Am I doing the right thing?" Kara asked.

Atlin sighed and said, "Well, let's see. You are risking your life, going into the unknown, to try to find something that may save your people. A people, who have treated you like dirt your entire life. No matter how this turns out, I'd say you're doing the right thing."

Kara looked around and finally realized Gallus was no where to be seen. It was so unusual to see her father without his royal guard close beside him.

"Where is uncle Gallus?" Kara asked.

"He's preparing the defenses." Atlin answered. "First time we haven't been in eye sight of each other in thirty-five years. I see your royal guard is somewhere else as well. Feel's funny, doesn't it? Like a piece of you is somewhere else?

Kara nodded as Atlin put his arm around her.

"I would've liked to say goodbye." Kara said.

"He knows you love him."

Atlin had always wondered why Kara started calling Gallus by rank. He felt this was as good a time to ask.

"Why did you start calling your uncle, general?" he asked.

Kara had to think about the question herself. It had become such a habit over the years that she couldn't even remember when she started it. However, she did remember *why* she started doing it. It was the same time she stopped calling her her father "daddy."

The Goddess

"I wanted to be more grown up." Kara answered. "Do you remember when I started?"

Atlin sighed and said, "How could I forget? It was during your two years in the city. Your uncle looked like he got punched in the gut all day."

Kara closed her eyes feeling terrible. She never thought about how much she might be hurting him by distancing herself so.

Atlin looked down at the weapon in Kara's hand. He was somewhat surprised at how well kept it looked. He expected the dust and lack of oil to have rusted the blades by now.

"I remember when you first presented that to the council. For the record, I thought it was a good idea." he told her.

"I remember you almost beat me with that." a feminine voice said.

Both Atlin and Kara looked over at the doorway to see Delia standing there.

"Almost being the key word." Kara quoted her father.

Delia came in and took a seat next to her father. The three of them sat there in silence, taking in the moment. They knew this could be the last time they would ever be together. Atlin puts his arms around his girls and held them tight. He kissed them on their heads as tears welled up in his eyes.

"My strong brave girls." Atlin began. "I love you."

"We love you too, daddy." Kara whispered as tears rolled down her cheeks.

Delia threw her arms around her father with a smile and said, "I'm not going to cry but I love you too, dad."

Atlin chuckled at his youngest's bravado. The girl always tried to be tough and covered her insecurities with humor. Of the two of them, Kara had always been the more emotional. He couldn't even remember the last time he'd seen Delia cry.

Delia pulled back and said, "We have to go. We'll be back soon."

"Bye dad." Kara said as she quickly walked out the door, wiping her tears, and without looking back.

Delia followed Kara but unlike her sister, she smiled and waved at her father as she left the room.

Atlin let out a deep breath and laid back on the bed as his daughters left. It was time to get to business.

****

General Bellus entered the city of Voya to find that it was nearly empty. Most of the people had fled to the capital of Andor already with the unlucky few being captured or slaughtered by the men. It didn't matter, there was no where to hide from the Numeran army. Eventually, the army would make its way to Andor. There would be no where to run at that point except for the Arctic Sea. From what Bellus understood, the Khalians had no operational ships to escape with. Unless someone wanted to get into a small fishing boat and take their chances on the frigid waters, the slaughter was inevitable.

The battle had been an embarrassment for Khalia. Bellus couldn't even call it a battle. The Khalians had no archers defending the walls. All Numera had to do was walk up to the walls, deploy their ladders, and walk on up. The disadvantages for Khalia didn't stop with their lack of archers. They were poorly trained and knew nothing of warfare. Their equipment was even worse. From where Bellus had been commanding, he saw countless times where Numerans swords would punch straight through Khalian shields and kill the man trying to defend himself. The Khalians might as well have been using wax shields from the ancient days.

"General, the city is secured. What are your orders?" a captain asked.

"Prepare the men. We march north." Bellus told him.

Usually, Bellus would order that the city be fortified in case of a counter-attack. However, Bellus doubted the Khalians could put up much of a fight even if they decided on this course. Also, the thought of Decimus hadn't escaped Bellus' mind. He had to beat Decimus to Andor's gates.

After seeing the "resistance" the Khalians put up, Bellus

was feeling a little better about the fate of the men Decimus commanded. Even if Decimus arrived at Andor first, he doubted the Khalians could cause much damage. However, Bellus didn't want to take the chance. The Khalians could be smart enough to have a surprise for them. He wanted to be there first and prevent Decimus from doing something stupid and getting the men killed.

"We have incoming!" a soldier shouted from the walls.

Bellus got off his mount and headed up the steps of the walls. He doubted a counter-attack could happen so soon. They had only attacked Voya a few hours ago. If the Khalians defending Voya had sent a rider to warn Andor, it would take at least a day for the rider to arrive.

As Bellus got to the top of the walls, he observed a small group heading their way. The men carried a Khalian banner, but the force was not enough for a counter-attack. Neither did they look to be ready for battle. They may have been sent to reinforce Voya but weren't aware that the city was already taken.

Are they this stupid? Bellus wondered.

Smoke was rising from Voya. Although the battle had been short, there were still buildings that were on fire. Surely, the Khalians could see this but they just kept marching forward. Either these men were incredibly brave, or they were too stupid to realize their city had fallen. Bellus thought the latter more likely since none of the Khalians seemed to be ready for combat. They marched as if they were ready to get within the city's walls and take a rest.

"Prepare the cavalry." Bellus ordered. "Charge the men, capture any who surrender."

"As you will, General." the captain next to him said.

Bellus watched for any changes to the men coming towards the walls. The Khalians had to know that they couldn't beat Numera using conventional means. This could be some elaborate trap to draw the Numerans out into the open field.

Within minutes, the horn sounded to signal the charge.

A single division of horsemen should be enough. It would also give Bellus a chance to see what the Khalians were up to, should this be a trap.

As the cavalry thundered out into the open field, Bellus held his breath at what could potentially happen. If the Khalians were setting a trap, Bellus might have just sent a hundred men to their deaths. Luckily, for Bellus and the Numeran horsemen, the Khalians began to panic. Most of them broke ranks and immediately ran for their lives at the sight of the Numeran horses coming at them. The Khalian captain tried to organize some semblance of an effective fighting force. However, by this time, the captain's men weren't even listening.

The Numeran horses charged straight into this disorganized mess the Khalians called soldiers. Men went flying through the air, as did body parts and blood. One or two brave men tried to fight back by taking out a horses' legs but even these courageous souls were cut down almost immediately by another mounted warrior. The men who had fled were easily chased down, their feet unable to run fast enough to avoid the horses charging after them.

Despite their ineffectiveness, none of the Khalians who had stayed to fight, surrendered. They continued to at least try until the bitter end. The Khalians clearly knew the fate that awaited them if they surrendered to the Numerans. Bellus himself couldn't blame them. Any Khalian who was captured was not going to be conscripted into the army. There were no other enemies to fight after this small pathetic nation. Emperor Gradus would most likely have them executed quickly if they were lucky. If the Emperor was looking for entertainment, that execution would be incredibly slow.

As the "battle" came to a close, Bellus could see that none of the Khalians had survived. A few of his men were injured but there was no one with black armor lying on the battlefield.

The Khalians really are that stupid. Bellus thought.

Of all the battles he'd seen, the cities he'd sacked, and the nations he'd conquered, Bellus had never had such an easy time of it. He began to wonder how a nation such as this produced a warrior like Delia. At the same time, their greatest warrior was a woman. Perhaps that was saying something about these people.

"General, the Emperor brings word." a messenger said as he handed Bellus a note.

Bellus read the note from the Emperor saying that he wanted to be present when Andor fell. Clearly, the Emperor wanted to be there for the final battle. The fall of Andor would consolidate his power over the entire world. This was actually good news for Bellus.

This entire time, Bellus had been racing against the clock. He was concerned about making it to Andor's walls before Decimus did. Now that the Emperor wished to be present, it would force Decimus to hold his position until the rest of the army had reached the walls as well.

Bellus grabbed a messenger near him and ordered, "Go northwest and wait for Decimus and his forces. The Emperor wishes to be present during the final battle. Tell Decimus that if he attacks the city before the Emperor arrives, it will be his head."

The messenger hesitated for a second. He did not relish having to deliver a threat to the "demon." Seeing this, Bellus wrote down what he had just said onto a piece of paper and handed it to the messenger.

"Just hand this to him. Get away from him before he reads it." Bellus said to the boy.

Decimus had been known to take his frustrations out on his own men. Bellus didn't want to imagine what Decimus would do to the boy.

It would take time to organize and move the entire camp to Andor's walls. However, it was now time that Bellus had. After the showing today, the Khalians didn't seem to be much of a threat. No matter how the Khalians prepared the city, Bellus was certain the battle and this entire war would be over soon. He wondered what he would do once it was all over. Perhaps he would go back to Numera and have a quiet life in the countryside. He looked forward to the peace after a lifetime of war. Whatever he did, he was determined to give Nola and her child a good life. One where she wouldn't feel like a slave.

****

Kara and Delia raced their horses as fast as they could outside the city walls. When they were younger, these used to be fun little distractions. It was the one physical activity Kara stood a chance against Delia in. Of course, Delia would always argue that it didn't count since the horse was doing most of the work. It seemed like now, all the fun was gone. They weren't racing against each other. They were racing against time. Each second could mean the difference between the nation surviving and its utter destruction.

As the two girls arrived at the dock, they saw that Aurin and the men had already prepared the ship to depart. The dock itself was quite small. It was used by fishing boats during the summer when the waters were warmer. The Arita looked somewhat misplaced in such a small dock. The ship wasn't that big but compared to the small boats that usually docked here, it looked massive.

The twenty men that were working on the ship were the same ones who accompanied Kara in Imbor. They were the few who supported Kara and that support changed to reverence after the Battle of Imbor. They had seen how the princess led, how she fought, and how she brought hope to the people even when death was inevitable. Just like Aurin, many of them thought this journey was folly. However, Kara was their beloved princess and they would follow her even if nothing came of this.

Aurin came up and greeted the two girls. From the look on his face, Kara could see that the man had been worried. If something were to happen to Kara and he wasn't there, he would never be able to forgive himself. Kara had to smile at the man's dedication as well as the fact that he cared about her so much.

The Goddess

"I see you survived." Kara teased.

Aurin just shook his head and said, "Never again."

Kara and Delia just looked at each other and chuckled. As they got ready to board the ship, everyone was surprised to find someone riding up to the dock on a horse. Looking closer, they could see that it was Lieutenant Gidor. Aurin glared at the man as he dismounted and came closer. Aurin gripped the hilt of his sword, ready to protect the princess should Gidor try anything to stop them.

Surprisingly, Gidor came with his own bag draped across his back. He made no hostile move as he slowly strode towards the three friends.

"I'm coming with." Gidor announced as he got closer.

Nobody knew what to say. They just wondered why Gidor decided to come in the first place. Everyone knew how he felt about Kara. It was strange that he was leaving Khalia in its time of need to pursue something that might turn out to be utter fantasy.

"The hell you are." Aurin began.

Gidor calmly turned to the man and said, "Does anyone in your small company know how to sail? I was born and raised near the docks. You need me."

Aurin gritted his teeth at Gidor's argument. It was true. Before Kara and Delia arrived, the men were desperately trying to figure out how to work the Arita. They weren't sailors. Some of them had never been on a ship before in their entire lives. They decided to just finish loading the supplies onboard and figure out the rest later.

The four of them began walking towards the deck of the ship. Kara began to wonder how Gidor had even found out about the journey. She didn't need to ask as Gidor immediately explained everything.

"General Yusa told me you were taking the Arita before he left." Gidor said.

"Has the general already taken his men towards Nabu?" Delia asked.

"Yes, but everyone knows it's futile. His mission is to slow the advancing army in the southwest, not to stop it." Gidor answered.

Kara grimaced at the thought. General Yusa was being sent on a suicide mission. It was necessary to give Andor time to prepare its defenses as well as provide cover to the fleeing refugees. However, Kara also knew the chances of Yusa or his men surviving this was slim.

"How long is the journey?" Gidor asked.

Kara pulled out the parchment with the map on it and handed it to Gidor.

"The map says it's three days north." Kara answered. "That was centuries ago, though. We have faster ships now and the Arita is the fastest. She was designed for speed."

"Good." Gidor replied. "We'll have to act as fast as possible."

As soon as Gidor stepped onto the deck, he began issuing orders as if he were in command. Once again, Aurin moved to put the man in his place. However, Kara put a hand on Aurin's shoulder to stop him.

"He's the only one that knows what he's doing with the ship." Kara explained. "Let him."

Aurin just gritted his teeth once again. He really did not like Gidor. From the moment Aurin met him nearly a decade ago, Gidor had always been arrogant. He always thought he was right and took charge when it suited him. The fact that Gidor did not restrain himself when it came to talking about Kara only served to further anger Aurin.

"Alright! Everything's set!" Gidor announced. "Let's go."

Gidor took his position at the helm as the ship creaked at being moved for the first time in months. Delia hadn't been on a ship since she was ten. She never liked the rocking movement of the deck and braced herself as she knew it would only get worse on the open water.

Kara went over to the rear of the ship. Behind the helm was a plaque for the Arita. She placed her hand on the cold metal as she stared at the ship's namesake.

Kara closed her eyes and whispered a silent prayer, "Mom, I wish I could've known you. I don't know if you can hear me or if you're here with us now. Please don't let this journey be in vain. I love you."

As Kara left, Gidor worked to navigate the ship into the open water. He had heard the princess' prayer. He didn't know whether the queen was with them either. However, he did wish the same thing Kara did. If this journey was in vain, it could mean the end of his beloved country.

CHAPTER 7

Kara leaned against the bow of the ship, taking in the wind as it whipped her hair into the air. The nice clean air reminded her of the times along the cliffs. It seemed so peaceful out on the open water. She didn't have to think of anything else besides the unending water in front of her. That peace was interrupted from time to time as Delia puked over the sides of the ship. Kara chuckled to herself seeing her sister like this. The always strong and mighty Delia was reduced to ejecting her insides due to some rocky waters.

"Delia, you alright?" Kara teased.

Delia didn't say anything but the hand gesture she gave told Kara to shut up and leave her alone. Kara laughed and looked over to Aurin who was trying to hold in a chuckle himself.

The poor girl never did like being on the water. When Delia was ten years old, their father and taken the two girls out on a fishing boat. Delia was so excited about being on a boat for the first time in her life. That excitement was short-lived. Within half an hour, the girl immediately began puking all over the deck. Their father had no choice but to turn the boat around and take them back to the docks. It was fine by Kara. She'd always found fishing to be boring. Delia swore she would never step foot onto the open ocean again. Seems, she never got over her seasickness.

As Kara turned back around to stare out at the water, Gidor came up and leaned against the bow beside her. He didn't say anything or even look at her. He just took a deep breath of the cool air. Aurin took a step towards them but Kara gestured with her hand that it was alright.

"So, tell me something, princess." Gidor began. "Why do you fight?"

"Why do you?" Kara asked.

"Because Khalia is my home. I fight to defend my friends and family."

Kara laughed and asked, "You don't think I have friends and family?"

"Don't get me wrong. I understand that. However, you fight for the well-being of the people. That's what I don't get. Why do you even care so much about them? They've treated you like garbage your entire life."

"Sometimes I wonder myself." Kara took a deep breath before continuing. "You're a leader. What if your commander told you to sacrifice yourself to save me? Would you do it?"

Gidor looked at Kara and hesitated before saying, "Sometimes, as soldiers, we don't get to choose our mission."

"There you go." Kara said. "I was born a princess. I don't get to choose who I serve and don't. I serve my country. I serve her people. Despite everything I've suffered, I still love them. I would do anything for them."

Gidor chuckled and said, "Despite popular belief, princess, I don't hate you."

This was surprising to Kara. Gidor had always treated her like an outcast. He never said anything horrible to her in person, but she heard from other people what he would say when she wasn't there. Usually, the man would avoid her or give her hostile glances from across the room.

"I always felt you were a spoiled child." Gidor explained. "Sure, you went through hardships but who hasn't? Then, six months ago, you demanded command of a military force despite the fact you had no military training. I thought you were playing at soldier. Playing with the lives of men."

Kara prepared to defend herself. Those same men were on the ship with them at this moment. She hadn't been playing with anyone's live then and definitely not now.

"But then, I spoke with them." Gidor said. "I know what you did in Imbor, princess. I still think this mission is a long shot. I never believed you were the incarnation of Yalka. However, I do believe you want what's best for your people. That's someone who I can follow and that's why I'm here now."

Gidor smiled at Kara and left the girl standing there in surprise. She never thought a man like Gidor could ever come around to respecting her. Yet, here he was, telling her that he would follow her for the sake of the nation. It was a step. Perhaps one day, Gidor could even come to trust Kara. Perhaps they could even become friends.

Kara laughed at herself at the thought. The last one was such a huge stretch.

Let's just take it one step at a time. Kara thought.

"Land!"

Kara as well as everyone else looked up at the crow's nest. The lookout up top was pointing towards the horizon. Kara looked out only to see ice. She didn't see land anywhere. Suddenly, she felt the ship adjusting its direction towards the ice. Kara ran over to the helm where Gidor had taken his place again.

"What land? All I see is ice." Kara said.

"That's definitely land. You can tell the difference from the crow's nest." Gidor explained.

Kara had her doubts, but she trusted the men knew what they were doing. If not, they'd find out very quickly. You didn't have to see an experienced sailor to know that being trapped in an ice field was the last thing you wanted.

"Get the boat ready!" Gidor shouted.

The men worked to prepare the small rowboat that would take Kara and a few of her companions onto the shore. Delia finally pulled her head from the side of the ship and she came over to Kara.

"Oh, thank Yalka." Delia groaned.

Kara chuckled and asked, "You good to go?"

Delia just gave a thumbs up. She still looked sick, but Kara was confident the girl would feel better once she had some solid ground under her feet.

"You realize it's only been a day." Aurin said.

Kara looked at the parchment map. As the ship got closer, she could make out the features of the small island. It was covered in snow but now that they were close, she could tell that it was definitely land. The details on the map were striking. There was no doubt this was the island they were looking for.

"Guess our ships have improved since Isa's day." Kara said.

"How did he even find this place?" Delia asked.

"Who knows. Maybe Yalka led him." Kara said with a chuckle.

"Whatever. I just want to get off the ship." Delia said.

This was it. Kara closed her eyes and took a deep breath. If they couldn't find what they were looking for on this island, everything was for naught. They would know the fate of Khalia within a few hours.

****

General Yusa could see the smoke from Nabu now. He and three-hundred men had already passed many refugees fleeing from the burning city. They told horror stories about what the Numerans had done. Yusa let these people speak, hoping the atrocities they spoke of would galvanize his men to fight harder when they met the enemy. Unfortunately, this didn't go as planned.

Some the refugees had said that the "demon" was leading the Numerans they were about to face. This "demon" was dismissed as a rumor by the war council. Only a few, including the princess, took these rumors seriously. According to accounts, this "demon" who went by the name of Decimus, was invincible. He wasn't a man but a suit of armor that was possessed by a specter from hell.

The men began to panic after hearing the survivors tell their tales. They wanted to turn back and forget about engaging the Numerans. It was only after Yusa spoke to the men about the consequences of abandoning their mission that they continued to march.

He had told them, "Think about your families back in Andor. Think about the families of Nabu. If we turn back now, they will all suffer. You are the heroes of this nation. No one else will fight this evil. So, you decide. I will not stop anyone who turns back now."

Luckily, the men knew what was at stake. They began to march once again. Yusa was actually hoping some of them would turn back. This was a suicide mission and he knew it. He commended the men's bravery to continue their march to death. However, he also prayed for a miracle because they needed one. Not just to survive the battle ahead them but to survive as a nation.

Before long, the number of survivors they encountered began to dwindle. Yusa's heart pounded in his chest as he caught sight of the army that had taken Nabu. It looked like a swarm of black ants, ready to devour anything that stood in their way. However, Yusa could also see that it wasn't the main army. They were not marching in formation nor did they have any archers or cavalry. Although the Numerans dwarfed his own forces in comparison, there was still a chance to do much damage to them and slow them down significantly.

Yusa stopped his own men and rode out in front of them.

"Men of Khalia, hear me!" Yusa began. "What do you see in front of you?"

The men were scared. They could only see death standing on the horizon.

"Those are the bastards that killed our people!" Yusa continued. "They have raped our women, killed our children. Their very presence here stains the land with their evil. You are the cure! Go and wreak vengeance in the name of Khalia! For Khalia!"

"For Khalia!" the men screamed in unison as they charged forth.

The Numerans did not expect to encounter a Khalian force before making it to Andor. They had been slaughtering civilians up to this point. As the Khalians charged at them, they drew their weapons and realized they were unprepared.

Galvanized by their general's speech and seeing the Numerans had been caught by surprise, the Khalians charged with such ferocity that it shocked the encroaching army. Several of the Numerans fell as they fumbled to draw their weapons. Despite the size of the Numeran forces, they began to panic at the sheer aggressiveness the Khalians were unleashing upon them. Blood and bodies began to litter the snow-covered ground at their feet. The small Khalian force was pushing the Numerans back.

Yusa sat on his mount assessing the situation. He couldn't believe what he was seeing. His small force was actually winning. The Numerans were in a panic. Hope began to swell in his heart. They could stop this force before it reached Andor's gates.

Unfortunately, this small success was short-lived. The Numerans had regrouped and began to fight back against the Khalians. No one was fighting in formation. The battlefield looked like a free-for-all. Everyone was hacking and slashing away at whatever was in front of them. Some of the men began fighting their own side, unable to distinguish friend from foe. In the middle of this carnage stood a giant. Yusa couldn't call him a man. His armor covered every part of his body. He held weapons too large for any man to wield. It was the demon, Decimus.

Decimus flung himself at the Khalians with ease. He would throw the men, two sometimes three at a time, across the battlefield. Some of the braver Khalians charged at him as a group, hoping to overwhelm him with numbers. The demon only laughed at their efforts as he slaughtered them like animals. The battle was lost. The very presence of the demon assured it.

"General, you should flee." Yusa's lieutenant, who stood next to him, suggested.

Yusa and a few of his officers were the only ones who had not entered the battle yet. He looked out at his men who were screaming and dying. With a deep breath, Yusa got off his horse. He handed the reigns to his lieutenant and told him, "It wouldn't be right. My men die because of my orders. I will die with them. You go to Andor and warn them."

The young lieutenant hesitated, reluctant to leave his brave and honorable general. He looked around at the other officers who gave him a nod to proceed. They had all made up their minds to die with the men they led. As the lieutenant got on the horse and proceeded to ride, he took one last look back, just in time to see the general draw his own sword.

"Gentlemen, we enter the fray! Tonight, we shall dine in the court of Yalka!" Yusa announced as the remaining men charged onto the battlefield.

Their general joining them lifted the morale of the Khalians once again. They watched as their brave leader cut through the Numerans who dared challenge him. The Khalians once again rallied behind their leader and began to push the Numerans back. The disorganized Khalian mess formed together to become a wave of death with Yusa at the vanguard.

As Yusa continued to cut down anything in black armor, he felt a dark presence block the shining sun behind him. He turned to see the massive suit of armor that was the demon as it bore down onto him. The demon swept his arm and threw Yusa to the ground. Yusa felt like he had been hit with a battering ram rather than the arm of a person. He struggled to get to his feet, but the demon stomped on his chest, crushing the ribs underneath his armor. Yusa screamed as the demon towered above him and grabbed his cheeks. The demon extended his right arm as a blade shot out from the wrist. Finally, the demon spoke. It was voice unlike any Yusa had ever heard. It was deep and guttural. Yusa couldn't even say it was human.

"How disappointing." Decimus said. "I was hoping for more of a fight. Before you die, know that your suffering is only the beginning for your people."

With that, Decimus shoved the wrist blade into Yusa mouth and began cutting his tongue out. The screams of the general echoed across the noisy battlefield. The Khalians lost the will to fight at the sight of their leader, suffering as this demon defiled him. Many of them turned around and ran. Some of them dropped their weapons in fear, making them easy targets for other Numerans. Soon, Yusa's screams became choked gurgles as blood pooled in his mouth. When Decimus was satisfied, he reached into the bloody mouth of the man and with one strong pull, yanked the general's tongue out. He held his trophy and bellowed out a cry of triumph.

The battle was over. All around, Khalians were either running for their lives or being cut down. None had the will to fight any longer. Decimus surveyed the scene as he attached his newly acquired tongue onto his belt. The snow was glistening a bright red from all the blood. This was what Decimus lived for. He was eager to get more of it.

****

Bellus was in his tent, busy packing his own belongings as the entire camp got ready to move out. Nola was beside him, helping to pack as well. Being a slave, the girl didn't have much in the way of personal items. However, there was a spoon she was rather fond of. It took a while for Bellus to get the entire story out of the girl, but she eventually told him.

In the slave section of the camp, the slaves were given utensils from a shared supply. These were barely ever washed so one can imagine how much disease was spread from just using the utensils to eat. Nola had stolen a spoon for her own use and held onto it. If she were ever found out, it would be a death sentence. Bellus was glad the girl was comfortable enough to share this with him. She could've been handing him an excuse to execute her.

"This will be the last battle. After this, we can go back to Numera." Bellus told her.

"Will I be living with you, master?" Nola asked.

"Yes. You and your child."

Nola hesitated before asking, "What if I wish to go

home?"

"To Anaya?"

Bellus thought for a second. He didn't want to force the girl to stay if she didn't want to, but he hated to lose a friend. He also knew Anaya wouldn't be the same under Numeran rule. He struggled with himself with whether to tell her the truth. He decided she had to know.

"I won't stop you from going back home but you should know it'll be different. It won't be a nice place. Especially for an Anayan woman." Bellus explained.

Nola took the information in. She knew the best place for her would be with Bellus. Her home wasn't there anymore. Going back would be inviting slavery again. This time, she might not be so lucky.

"Will I be taken as your wife, master?" Nola asked.

"No." Bellus answered.

"Because I'm a slave?"

Bellus stopped packing and looked at her. He sighed and said, "Because you're a woman."

Bellus didn't know why he had told her this. The girl now had something to use against him should she wish. All she had to say was that Bellus enjoyed the company of men and his entire life would be upturned. Still, the girl had trusted him with the story of the spoon. It was only right that he trust her with something.

From the girl's reaction, she didn't seem too surprised. During their conversations, he had often talked about some of the men he had served with. He spoke of them affectionately. Bellus never had any relations with them but perhaps the girl caught onto something.

"Just one more battle." Bellus said to her. "Then, we can live in peace."

Nola smiled and nodded.

As Bellus picked up his bag, he was surprised when the girl embraced him. Besides sleeping besides each other on the same bed at night, they never had any physical contact with each other. It was a pleasant surprise and Bellus found himself using his free arm to hug her back.

When they broke apart, Nola said, "Just be careful out there. Bellus."

Bellus smiled as his name rolled off the lips of the woman. He was glad to hear his friend call him by name. The smile didn't leave his face as he exited the tent and proceeded to his horse, ready to lead the men on their final march. It would be over soon.

CHAPTER 8

King Atlin adjusted the belt along his armor for the tenth time. He hadn't worn the armor in years. It chafed in spots and Atlin was embarrassed to admit he'd put on quite a few pounds over the years. Gallus had joined him earlier after the general had finished his preparations for the coming battle. The man had caught Atlin trying to squeeze into the armor that was a few sizes too small. Gallus had chuckled to himself watching his friend struggle.

As the two men made their way to the throne room, Atlin was still struggling to adjust to the feel of the armor around his body. Gallus had suggested going down to the blacksmith a few months before. Atlin had always put it off and was now regretting that decision. The last thing he wanted was to take a Numeran sword to the chest just because he was having trouble moving in the armor.

Atlin walked over the throne and stood in front of it. He wondered if he would ever sit in this chair again. As he let out a long sigh, Gallus walked up to Atlin, holding the king's helmet.

"It's better to do it quickly." Gallus said.

Atlin nodded as he removed the crown from his head and placed it on the seat of the throne. He had never taken off the crown outside of his room before. For the past twenty-five years, since his coronation as king, no one besides Gallus and his late wife had seen him without his crown. He couldn't even remember his daughters seeing him without the crown. As his mind wandered to his daughters, he wondered where they were at the moment.

Gallus handed the king his helmet as the two men walked

The Goddess

towards the front doors. Before they could leave, the doors opened, and a man entered. The sudden light from outside blinded the men momentarily. It was only after the man spoke, did they recognize who he was.

"I see you've gained a bit of weight, Your Highness."

Atlin blinked through the light and said, "Miru?"

As his eyes adjusted, Atlin could clearly see his dear old friend. It had been years since the two had seen each other. Atlin could see the man had aged but he still had the same friendly face. The king went over and embraced the man. If it hadn't been for Miru speaking out against Tula on the day Kara was born, Kara may not have survived at all. Atlin owed Miru his eldest daughter's life.

As the two men broke their embrace, Miru patted the front of Atlin's armor and said, "The armor looked less tight on you the last time I saw you put it on."

Atlin chuckled and said, "I'm not the only one who gained weight it seems."

Miru laughed, knowing age had affected them both around the waist. Miru looked towards Gallus and said, "It's good to see you again, friend."

Gallus smiled and gave a respectful nod to the man.

"So, how is it in exile?" Atlin asked.

It had been years since Miru was transferred to the church outside the city walls. Apparently, speaking out against the Archbishop wasn't the best way to rise up through the ranks of the church. Atlin offered Miru a place in the royal palace but the other priests had threatened to strip Miru of his position if he accepted. Having always been a man of faith, Miru decided this "exile" was preferable to not being in service to Yalka.

"It has its perks. Kara comes to see me all the time. Delia, not so much. Yalka knows that girl needs to go to church." Miru joked.

Atlin chuckled and asked, "What are you trying to say about my youngest?"

Miru laughed as he responded, "Just that the girl needs to

work on her spiritual side as much as her fighting skills."

"I'm glad you came into the city. You'll be safer here." Atlin said.

"Actually, you can thank Kara for that. She convinced me to take shelter inside the walls."

"Don't think I don't know that it was you who told her about this journey she's on."

Miru gave a sly grin and asked, "Are you mad at me, friend?"

Atlin smiled and replied, "Of course not. It keeps the girls away from the danger approaching."

Miru chuckled and said, "Knowing them, they'll be back before the battle is over."

Just then, the alarm bells around the city began to ring. The men's smiles disappeared as they realized what the bells were signaling. The enemy had been sighted on the horizon. They knew about the force approaching from the southwest, in the direction of Nabu. However, they never received word from Voya. Atlin wondered if Voya had even been attacked yet. He would find out in a moment.

"Go down into the city. You'll be safe there." Atlin told Miru.

Miru nodded as the three men headed out the door. Atlin and Gallus got on their mounts and quickly made their way to the walls of the first ring. As they got to the gate, they dismounted their horses and climbed the steps to the top of the wall. General Sulin and Tula were at the top of the wall as well. Everyone was staring out into the horizon but no one was saying anything.

As Atlin looked out towards the southwest, he could see a small force out on the horizon. The black armor gave their allegiance away. The Numerans who had sacked Nabu had arrived. It looked like General Yusa had done a better job than anyone could have anticipated. Although the size was still formidable, the force was small and disorganized. They were still too far away for anyone to make out details, but it was clear this was not the main army.

Just then, the men at the gate began shouting, "Open the gate! Rider incoming!"

As the gate opened, a young lieutenant rode in and quickly dismounted his horse. He ran up to the wall and saluted the king, exhausted and out of breath.

"Your Highness, General Yusa has fallen. There are still refugees out there. The Numerans are chasing them down and killing them. One other thing, my Lord. The force approaching the gates now is being led by the demon." the lieutenant reported.

Atlin looked out across the field again. He saw small black figures breaking off from the larger horde and chasing after separate figures in front of them. Atlin couldn't make out what it was at first. After the lieutenant's explanation, Atlin realized it was the Numerans killing the civilians.

"Forget about them. They're dead anyway." Tula said coldly.

Atlin glared at the man before shouting, "Prepare three divisions! Send them out to cover the people!"

The Khalians immediately did as the king ordered.

"Your Highness, this is futile!" Tula said.

"Enough, priest! Those are our people out there!" Atlin yelled.

"Did you not hear? The demon leads them!" Tula argued.

Atlin chose to ignore Tula this time. It didn't matter to the king if the devil himself were out there. The only thing that mattered was protecting his people.

"You would risk us all to save those too weak to flee?" Tula persisted.

Atlin finally turned to Tula and calmly said, "Get off my wall before I throw you off of it."

Tula did not argue any further. The way the king looked at him as he said this sent a cold chill up his spine. Tula immediately left the wall before the king made good on his threat.

"General Sulin, give me a report of our forces." Atlin ordered.

"Every man, woman, and child has been given arms, Your Highness." Sulin began. "The women and children have been placed inside the inner walls. The better trained men have been placed along the outside. Many of the teenage boys have volunteered to be part of the defenses. They're not well trained but eager to defend their home. Basically, the entire city has been militarized. If the Numerans take Andor, they will need to pay for it with blood."

"Has there been any word from Voya?" Gallus asked.

"None. We must assume Voya has been taken." Sulin answered.

"Agreed." Atlin said. "Let's just hope the main army takes its time. We need to get as many of those people into the city as we can."

Three divisions of three-hundred men were mobilized as the gates opened once again. The men quickly ran towards the southwest, ready to defend the people from the evil that was trying to slaughter them.

As Atlin watched from the walls, he prayed silently for the men who were now running towards the force on the horizon. Their mission wasn't to stop the enemy. It was to get the people to safety. Despite that, fighting eventually occurred. As the Numerans and Khalians drew closer together, an engagement was inevitable. Luckily, the Numerans didn't seem to know what they were doing. They charged at the Khalians in disorganized groups. Sometimes, a group of refugees would fall behind. A few brave Khalian soldiers would go after them, trying to protect them from the Numerans who ran towards them as sharks going towards a bloody piece of meat. Eventually, any semblance of order was gone from both sides. There were several groups on the battlefield, fighting each other without any sense of order. Luckily, this gave the refugees time to make it to the walls. However, it wasn't all of them. Some refugees were stuck amongst the fighting men, praying for a chance to run for safety.

The Goddess

Atlin witnessed the utter chaos that was ensuing. He could not call for a retreat without leaving those refugees out there to die. The good news was, the Khalians seemed to be holding their own for now. Despite the three-hundred men being divided across the battlefield, the small pockets of soldiers were doing a good job of surviving. As long as the Numerans were fighting them, the civilians would be safe. However, Atlin knew this wouldn't last forever. Eventually, the Numerans would overrun them and the civilians would die anyway.

Atlin looked to the sky and prayed again.

Whoever is listening, Yalka or whatever divine being is out there, please hear our pleas. We need a miracle.

****

The snow was different on the island than it was back in Khalia. It was snow that hadn't seen contact with humans for centuries. As the pure soft white powder crunched underneath Kara's boots, she took in the air and looked around the small quiet piece of land. The entire island was no more than a few hundred feet in either direction. Besides a few rock formations, it was completely barren. There were icebergs on the horizon bigger than the island itself.

Delia, Aurin, and Gidor were the only ones that came with Kara. The other men were told to stay on the ship and head back to Khalia if they did not return within a day. There was no way to know what they would find. They could find this "power" Isa had mentioned in his journals or they could meet their doom by some unknown force.

As Aurin tied their boat down to make sure it didn't float away, Kara looked down at the map to get some type of reference to where they should be going. Fortunately, Isa seemed to be meticulous when it came to detail. A large rock formation jutted out from the flat ground ahead of them. According to the map, they should be able to find a door there which led underground. Unfortunately, that was where the details ended. There was no telling what lay ahead afterwards.

The four of them quietly made their way to the rock formation. From just looking at it, there was no way to tell there was even a door or how to open it. They began touching the walls of the cold stone, brushing away at the snow, trying to find any indication of an entrance.

Delia gave out a loud sigh and asked, "You sure this is the way?"

Kara looked down at the map once again. She was positive this was the formation the map was talking about. It hadn't changed at all in the centuries since Isa was here.

"I'm positive." Kara answered.

As Kara ran her hands along the stone, she could feel it becoming colder to the touch. A part of the formation didn't feel like stone, it felt like metal. Just then, a glow emanated from the area where Kara's hand was placed, and the entire island began to rumble. Everyone drew their weapons preparing for whatever came their way. Kara held the map tightly in her left hand and gripped her bladed staff with her right.

Luckily, the rumbling wasn't an indication of anything hostile, it was the door sliding up and opening. The entrance led down a set of stairs. It was too dark to see anything below. Kara put the map back into her bag.

That's it for the map. Now, we're completely in the dark. Kara thought.

Kara chuckled to herself at the unintended pun as she stepped foot into the darkness, the others following close behind her. It led down to a straight corridor. The four of them froze again as they got to the bottom and the corridor lit up. It wasn't from torches but from what looked like small glass tubes. Kara tapped at one of the lighted tubes, fascinated by how they worked.

It wasn't the time to wonder about that now. They had to find a way to save their nation. Kara and her friends continued onward until they saw another door. This time, the door wasn't hidden. It was clearly a metal door, but it wouldn't open as they got close.

The Goddess

"Great. Are we going to spend the whole day finding ways to open doors?" Gidor asked sarcastically.

They tried pushing the door open. Aurin even tried to bash his shoulder against it, only to walk away sore. Kara stared at the rectangular object next to the door. Earlier, the stone outside had lit up when Kara ran her hands on it. Perhaps she could do the same here.

As soon as Kara's hand swept across the glass surface of this object, a sound emanated from it. Once again, everyone was on alert, but a green light shone from the rectangular object and the door began to rise up as it did outside.

"At least if we run into another door, we'll know what to do." Delia said.

There was no need for them to open anymore doors. The door led to their final destination. Everyone gasped aloud at what was in front of them. The room was larger than anything they had seen before. The walkway led to a circular platform which seemed to stand on air. All around them were lights and devices they had never even imagined could exist. To the four of them, it seemed like they had indeed entered the sanctuary of Yalka himself.

The circular platform had a large device in the middle, its purposes they could not even imagine. The platform itself seemed suspended in the air. Delia looked over the rail but couldn't even see the bottom. It was same when she looked above her. The room just seemed to go on endlessly.

As the four made their way to the middle of the platform, a woman appeared in front of them. At first, they all drew their weapons, but they realized that this wasn't a normal woman. She shone with a blue hue and looked as if made of light. Her features were absolutely flawless, more perfect than any human imaginable. She wore clothes they had never seen. She looked like a goddess.

Immediately, Delia, Aurin, and Gidor took a knee and bowed their heads wondering if they stood before a true deity. All except for Kara who looked upon the woman in fascination more than anything else. Kara was supposedly a goddess herself. Gods did not bow before other gods. At least that was what Delia was hoping. Otherwise, they would find out very quickly the limits of Kara's mortality if this goddess got offended.

"Welcome." the goddess greeted. "My name is Gia. How may I help you today?"

Kara looked around the room. She looked at the large device in the center of the platform and looked at Gia who smiled at her in an unnatural way. She looked at her friends behind her who dared not look up and be struck down by the figure in front of them. She began to understand what this place was.

"Guys, get up." Kara told the others.

The others slowly and carefully raised their heads. Their eyes were still on the goddess who called herself Gia. They didn't dare to offend her and suffer her wrath.

"It's a library." Kara said.

By now, the others got their feet and began looking around at the room once more at Kara's comment. They didn't understand what she was saying.

"How could this be a library?" Delia asked.

"Look around." Kara began. "Everything is separated into sections. Whatever is being kept is put into these devices and the device in the middle is to find what you're looking for."

It took a moment for the others to begin to comprehend what Kara was trying to explain. The walls were lined with man-sized containers, each of them made of a strange metal. There were strange words that they couldn't read separating each section. The large device in the middle had rectangular devices around it like the one Kara had interacted with at the door.

"What about her?" Gidor asked as he indicated towards Gia.

Kara turned to Gia and asked, "Gia, what are you?"

"I am the keeper of this vault." Gia began. "My purpose is to greet any visitors and provide them with information should they ask."

"She's a machine." Gidor said, feeling embarrassed he bowed down to it earlier.

"How could she be a machine? She's alive. She's interacting with us." Aurin argued.

"Gia, are you a machine?" Kara asked.

Gia looked a bit annoyed by the question before answering, "In a manner of speaking. I am an eighth-generation artificial intelligence created to manage, organize, and supplement the operations of this facility."

The other looked at Gia in puzzlement, not able to comprehend a word of what she just said.

Gia picked up on this and added, "Yes, a machine. Although, a fairly advanced one."

"Who created you?" Delia asked.

"I'm sorry. I do not have that information. Some of my memory banks have been corrupted over the long centuries." Gia answered.

The revelation was a lot to take in for the four friends standing there. This place had been here for centuries and someone created it. They didn't know if it was made by the hands of men or by gods. Either way, they were standing in a place they didn't fully understand, and it made them feel uneasy.

"Gia, do you know of a man named Isa?" Aurin asked.

"Ah, yes." Gia began. "He was the last person to enter this facility precisely six-hundred-two years ago. After asking a multitude of questions over the course of a day, he instructed me to close the doors and lock the facility to anyone trying to enter."

"How did *he* get in?" Delia asked.

"The door was open." Gia answered.

"Wait. If the doors were locked, why were we allowed to come in?" Kara asked.

"Because of you." Gia answered pointing at Kara. "As soon as you entered the facility, I was able to examine your biological structures and disallow entry. However, there was one among you who was able to bypass the locks."

"Why? What's different about me?" Kara asked.

"I do not know. My examinations of you seem to indicate you're the same as everyone else. However, there is something different I cannot understand." Gia answered.

"It's because you're a god." Delia said.

Kara felt a bit shaken by all this. For her entire life, Kara had always doubted her own divinity. Now, there was something removed from her own religious society that was saying there was something different about her. She didn't know how that made her feel, but it wasn't a pleasant feeling.

"Here's a better question." Gidor began. "Why are you taking instructions from us?"

The others didn't even consider this until Gidor had asked it. Gia admitted to having taken instructions from Isa when he came. She also answered every question they had asked thus far. Part of them wondered whether this was because she was created by their descendants and the history had been lost.

"Because it does not go against my programming." Gia answered.

"Your what?" Gidor asked having never heard the word before.

Gia gave an exasperated sigh. Kara found it quite humorous that this machine could feel such things and smiled to herself.

"My function." Gia clarified. "As I said, I was created to greet guests and provide information. I also have control over the doors and basic functions of this facility. That is the extent of my existence."

"Have we wasted our time?" Gidor asked the others. "There doesn't seem to be any weapon here."

"Maybe not." Kara answered. "Isa never said *weapon*. He said *power*."

"He also had a reason for locking the doors." Delia added.

Kara turned to Gia and asked, "What was the purpose of this place?"

"This vault was created to catalogue all diseases and

viruses of this world, both natural and artificial." Gia answered.

"Artificial? Why would you create a disease?" Aurin asked.

"To use it as a weapon." Gidor answered. "If you make the other side sick, it's as good as a weapon."

"Gia, we're being invaded by a force that outnumbers us. Is there anything in here that can help?" Kara asked.

"Perhaps." Gia answered.

The platform began to move upwards. The others recoiled at the sudden movement as the platform headed for its destination. When it stopped, a giant metal claw grabbed one of the man-sized containers off the wall. It brought the container to the large device in the center of the platform and placed it inside. A small door opened, and a glass tube the size of a person's palm came into view.

"This is an artificial virus called X-103. It was designed to be used as a weapon of mass destruction against an enemy force." Gia explained.

"What does it do?" Kara asked.

Gia answered, "Once it is exposed to open air, the virus goes airborne. It infects anyone within a three-kilometer radius. Within a matter of seconds, the virus will destroy the inhibition centers of the brain causing the infected to become incredibly violent to anyone in front of them. Within three hours, the subject will begin experiencing hemorrhaging within their internal organs. Basically, they will liquify from the inside out. Even after death, the virus will be highly contagious and near impossible to eradicate."

The four friends stood there in shock. They didn't understand much of what Gia said but they got the basic idea. This substance had the potential to kill everyone amongst the Numeran forces. It could change the tide of the war. It could save Khalia.

"I must warn you." Gia added. "Although I do not have much memory of the people who created this virus, I do know that they never employed it because they thought it too devastating. This substance has the potential to not only eliminate your enemies but the population of the world."

"We'll take the chance." Delia said as she approached the tube.

Kara put her hand on her sister's chest, stopping her from going further.

"Didn't you hear what Gia said? This could kill our people too." Kara argued.

"Our people are dead anyway if we don't use this!" Delia yelled.

"Kara, Delia's right." Aurin began. "There will be no Khalia if we don't use this."

"There will be no *world* if we use it!" Gidor added. "This is something we don't understand. People wiser than us restrained themselves from using it because of what it could do. We must follow their example."

The four of them looked at each other not knowing what to do. The situation was getting desperate. Each of them would do anything to save Khalia. Delia and Aurin wanted to save Khalia by any means necessary. Kara and Gidor knew that the entire world could be in jeopardy if they took this substance outside the vault.

Delia made the first move by pushing her way past her sister. Kara drew her staff and put it between Delia and the tube. Delia didn't say a word as she glared at Kara. She couldn't believe her sister was drawing a weapon against her. Delia hesitated for a second before drawing her own swords from her back and knocking Kara's staff away.

"Oh shit." Gidor said. "It just got real."

Aurin and Gidor drew their own swords as they stared each other down. The last time they went against each other was back in basic training nearly a decade ago. Aurin was always the victor then. More was at stake now. It wasn't just Khalia but the entire world on the line. Gidor was determined not to let the world suffer over a rash decision.

Delia went after Kara aggressively. The staff Kara developed was designed to quickly defend against such attacks. It was the reason why Kara had once almost beaten Delia during their sparring session. However, Delia was faster now, and Kara was having a hard time keeping up with her sister. As Kara kept getting pushed back, she could see Aurin and Gidor fighting each other out of the corner of her eye.

Gidor was having a hard time blocking Aurin's great sword. The great sword was slow but designed for power with each strike it landed. Gidor managed to block each incoming strike with his shield but he could feel his arm weakening. He wouldn't be able to keep this up. He needed to go on the offensive to stand any chance. As Gidor raised his shield above his head to block an overhead blow, he struck out with his sword, nicking the shin of Aurin.

Aurin cursed as he felt Gidor's sword cut into his leg. It was a superficial wound, but it could've been worse. He had forgotten how sly Gidor was in combat. The man would take every opportunity and advantage that was presented to him. Aurin realized he had to be more careful. That being said, strength was on his side. Gidor couldn't possibly keep up with the constant thundering of the great sword against his shield. Aurin began to swing away with all his strength, targeting the shield rather than trying to find a way around it.

The attacks worked. With a scream, Gidor fell to the ground. His arm behind the shield finally gave in as it broke behind the heavy strikes. Aurin stood over the man in victory.

Gidor chuckled and said, "You always were better."

Aurin looked over at Kara and Delia who were still busy fighting each other. Kara was getting exhausted whereas Delia looked like she was only just beginning. Delia moved inhumanly fast as she struck out against her sister. Kara knew she had to do something. She could no longer keep this up. As Kara was backed up into the railing of the platform, she saw it. Delia dropped her guard and left herself open. Kara drove her shoulder into Delia and managed to use her body weight to flip the smaller girl onto the floor. Delia lay there with Kara standing over her.

Something wasn't right in Kara's mind. It had been easy. Delia would never leave herself open. She looked over at Aurin who was standing in front of Gidor. She wondered if her own royal guard would attack her now. They stared at each other wondering how they got to this point. Four Khalians fighting one another – four friends.

Kara knelt down beside her sister and asked, "Why'd you let me win?"

Delia looked at Kara and said, "I didn't."

"I know how you fight, Delia!" Kara yelled. "I know you dropped your guard on purpose."

Kara stood back up and extended her hand to help Delia onto her feet. Aurin did the same to Gidor who took the man's hand with his good arm. The four friends looked at each other not believing what had just transpired. They had drawn their swords against each other over a weapon. If they needed confirmation for how evil this weapon was, they just got it.

"What the hell are we doing?" Kara asked.

"We can't win without it." Aurin said.

"No one wins with it." Gidor argued. "It's mutual destruction."

Nobody could argue with that. Both sides would be destroyed, and innocence would be caught in the middle. It wasn't a chance worth taking.

Just then, Gia interrupted and calmly asked, "Is your disagreement over?"

Kara ignored Gia as she turned towards her friends. She saw the hopelessness on their faces. They had come to find something to help them save Khalia. They were now going to leave empty-handed.

"We will find a way." Kara said. "We will save Khalia."

"How?" Delia asked.

"We'll keep fighting. It doesn't matter if it feels hopeless. We don't give up." Kara answered.

It wasn't the answer they wanted to hear. They all

wanted something specific, Kara included. However, it was all they could do. They couldn't give up. The only thing that mattered was moving forward.

Kara turned to Gia and asked, "Gia, is there anything else here that could help us? Something more conventional?"

"Perhaps." Gia answered.

This time, a moving image appeared before them. It surprised everyone at first. The picture looked as if it were made out of light. It was clear to see but you could also see what was on the other side of it. It had a similar appearance to the way Gia looked. Kara ran her hand through the image. There was nothing to feel. Her hand was touching the image, but it felt like the very air around them.

Gia continued her explanation, "This was meant to be the delivery system for the X-103. It is the only true weapon in this facility. It can be loaded with conventional explosive rounds, of which there are only eight. Would you like me to show you how to use it?"

"Show us how." Kara said.

CHAPTER 9

Bellus arrived at the walls of Andor only to see utter chaos to the southwest. Numeran and Khalian forces were fighting each other in scattered groups. Bellus couldn't believe the undisciplined mess that represented the Numeran forces. The Khalians were using the chaos to their advantage. They had managed to organize the fleeing refugees into small groups. As the scattered forces fought, the Khalians would use this as cover to send the refugees to the safety of Andor's gates. Decimus was nowhere to be seen.

Just what in the hell was that idiot doing? Bellus thought.

Decimus should've been commanding the Numerans to fight in an organized formation. The Numeran numbers far exceeded that of the Khalians. A disciplined fighting force moving forward could easily overtake the Khalians out on the field. Instead, the Numerans were charging at the Khalians at will, making their superior numbers obsolete. Bellus quickly grabbed a messenger nearest to him.

"Get to the southwestern forces. Tell them to stop engaging the Khalians and concentrate on forming an orderly formation. Surround a single group of refugees but do not kill them. Just keep them surrounded." Bellus relayed to the messenger.

Bellus' plan was to turn the Khalian's eagerness to save their people to the Numeran advantage. If they could surround just one refugee group and cut if off from reaching Andor's gates, the Khalians would continue to send forces to try to rescue them. Bellus hoped to drain the city of defenders this way. The final assault would then be much easier.

Bellus stopped the main army's march and ordered battle formations. Everything had to be in order before the final attack. The last thing Bellus needed was for everything to fall apart because they weren't organized. The first thing to do was to gain control of the mess in the southwest. Once the Khalians were sufficiently bled upon the open field, they could then march on the city and end this costly war.

****

King Atlin looked out over the horizon as the main Numeran army finally arrived. It was so much bigger than he could've imagined. There were literally thousands of them, their numbers beyond counting. Atlin felt fear for the first time since this battle had started, wondering how anything could stop such a force. Looking around the walls, Atlin could see that he wasn't the only one thinking such thoughts. Everyone's heart seemed to lose hope at the sight of the black swarm in front of them.

The good news at the moment was that the main army seemed to be holding position. They made no attempts to approach the city, although Atlin believed their sheer numbers alone would be sufficient to overwhelm the city's defenses. The bad news was that the Numeran forces in the southwest seemed to be getting more orderly now that their competent commander had arrived.

The Numeran forces in the southwest stopped charging at the Khalians wildly. Instead they pulled back and began to form ranks. They had surrounded a single refugee group and cut if off from escaping towards Andor's gates. The Khalians had already tried countless times to break the Numeran lines in order to get to the refugees and failed each time. Atlin sent out three more divisions, including one led by General Sulin, to try to force the Numerans to make a hole for the refugees.

Atlin was beginning to see the strategy of this cunning Numeran commander. Every other refugee group had made it to the walls except for the single trapped one. The Numerans were not trying to kill this group. They were being used as bait. Atlin had two choices at this point. Keep sending Khalian defenders out into the open field or bring everyone back inside the walls and leave the refugees to their fate. The latter option was the most strategic but monstrous as well. Atlin couldn't imagine leaving the innocent people to die but the more troops he sent out meant the less defenders there would be in the city when the real battle began.

Atlin didn't know what to do. This mind and heart her tearing at each other. Every part of his being was in debate over the right choice in this situation. Upon seeing another failure by the Khalian forces in trying to get to the refugees, Atlin had made his choice.

"Lieutenant." Atlin called to the man with the signal horn. "Call a…"

Before Atlin could finish the sentence, he saw something on the water. It was moving close to the fighting in the southwest. Atlin squinted to try to make out what it was. He could finally see the sails of a ship. His daughters had returned. The greatest warriors of Khalia had returned to join the battle. Atlin prayed they had something to turn the tide of this war.

****

Kara could see the assembled armies of Numera covering the land. The black armor they all wore was such a stark contrast to the white snow which covered the ground. She had seen something similar before, but it was months ago in Imbor. Now, the black death was on the doorsteps of her own home.

"Dear god." Aurin gasped as he looked out upon the black mass.

Aurin was thinking the same thing as everyone else on the ship. Just how were they going to stop something like that?

"Brace for impact!" Gidor yelled from the helm.

Everyone grabbed onto something as the Arita came at full speed right onto the beach. The journey from the island had taken less than a day this time. Luckily, they were traveling with the wind instead of against it. Some of the men on the ship liked to believe Yalka had changed the winds in their favor. Kara wasn't too sure but anything to help them get home faster was welcome in her eyes.

As the ship hit the beach, everyone hung onto anything they could get their hands on. The hull had ripped apart at the hard landing, but they weren't planning on leaving anytime soon. Once the rocking stopped, it was time to get to business.

Kara observed the battlefield and saw that the Numeran forces were split in two. The larger main army was to the city's south. They were still preparing their forces for the final assault on the city. The southwestern forces had already engaged the Khalians. It looked like a group of refugees were trapped behind the Numeran lines as the Khalians were bravely trying to get to them. It was time to help them out.

"Bring the weapon!" Kara called out.

Kara knew this weapon wouldn't do much in the long run. Gia had called it a mortar. She had shown them how to use it as well as demonstrating the destructive power of the weapon with the moving images. Unfortunately, they only had eight rounds. Once they had used all eight, the weapons would be useless unless they wanted to throw it at the enemy. Still, it could shock the Numerans into retreating temporarily and buy them some time to come up with another plan.

The men brought up the mortar and set it up on the ship's deck. Delia and Aurin carefully set it up and aimed it at the forces trapping the refugees. Hopefully, once the explosions began happening, it would scare the Numerans into breaking their formation and allowing the people to escape.

Gidor came down from the helm and strapped a shield to his broken arm. Kara couldn't believe Aurin had broken the man's arm during the fight. Gidor was a skilled warrior himself and they could've really used him without the handicap. Still, the man wasn't one to give up, even with an injury. He could probably best most of the Numerans even if both his arms were incapacitated.

"Alright, I think we're ready." Delia said.

"So, we just drop one of these in and it should shoot it out, right?" Aurin asked.

"That's what Gia said." Kara confirmed.

Aurin prepared one of the explosive rounds and dropped it down the barrel. Everyone looked at one another as nothing happened.

Are we missing something? Kara thought.

They waited for several seconds, wondering what they were doing wrong. They had done exactly as shown in the moving images as well as the instructions Gia had given. Could Gia have been mistaken? After all, she was created for the purpose of information, not combat.

"What are we doing wrong?" Aurin asked.

"Maybe we should take it out and try again?" Delia asked.

"No!" Kara yelled. "Gia said that could set if off."

"Well, then what do we do?" Delia asked in frustration.

As the three of them began arguing, Gidor walked up and kicked the weapon. With a loud pop, the round flew into the air and crashed into the Numeran lines with a loud explosion.

Gidor chuckled and said, "Machines are the same everywhere. Just kick them and they'll work."

Kara breathed a sigh of relief, thankful that they hadn't been blown up in the process. Aurin dropped another round down the barrel. This time, the weapon worked as intended as another round flew through the air and crashed into the Numerans. Pieces of men and armor exploded where the round landed.

The Numerans were panicking at this point. They didn't understand what they were being attacked with. Some of them began to wonder whether the gods themselves were attacking them from the heavens. A third round landed into their midst. This time, the Numerans began fleeing for their lives. All discipline broke within their ranks. As far as the Numerans were concerned, it was every man for himself at this point.

The Khalians were surprised as well but they also noticed the explosions were only targeting the Numerans. They could also see the trail of smoke each round left as it raced through the sky. Following it, they saw the Arita, beached on the shore and knew the attacks favored them. As the Numerans broke ranks, the Khalians took the opportunity to get the final group of refugees to safety. The Khalian soldiers under General Sulin held the line as the refugees were sent to Andor's gates with a small group of soldiers to defend them.

Despite most of the Numerans fleeing at this point, a small group broke apart from the larger mass and proceeded to chase the last group of refugees down. There was a group of about twenty Numerans running towards the civilians. There were only four Khalians defending the refugee group and it was clear they would be overrun. Seeing this, Delia jumped off the ship.

"I'm going after them!" Delia told the others.

Delia raced off in the direction of the refugees. They were only about a fourth of the way to the gate when the first of the Numerans reached them. The Numeran quickly cut down the first Khalian he encountered. The other Numerans had caught up and engaged two more of the Khalians. Both Khalians fell but not before taking four of the Numerans with them. Now there was only one Khalian soldier left to defend the civilians.

This "soldier" wasn't a soldier at all. He was just a small boy, his armor too big for his body. As the Numerans approached, he swung his sword wildly. His helmet kept coming down to cover his eyes, to which he had to stop swinging and adjust back onto his small head. It would have been a hilarious sight if not for the fact the boy was doing a good job of keeping the Numerans at bay. Despite having no experience or training, the boy had already taken down three Numerans who had approached him. By the time the fourth one fell, the other Numerans were having second thoughts about engaging this frail child.

As Delia got closer, she could she who this boy was. It was someone she had known since birth. She never thought she would ever see him in combat much less be so effective against men who were trained to fight and kill. It was Breka, the small and meek stable boy. The same boy who was picked on by his peers due to his size. The same one Gallus thought too inept to even enter basic military training.

The Numerans who had been chasing after the refugees began to fall back. It wasn't worth all the trouble to kill a few civilians. They also didn't want to get embarrassed by losing to such a small child. They all began to run back to the rest of their men. All except one large Numeran. This one didn't run towards the civilians. He was so big, each step he took was equal to four steps of a normal man. It was Decimus, the demon.

Breka stood his ground, determined to protect the innocent even if it meant his life. The demon suddenly charged at the boy and knocked him to the ground. Breka felt like he had been hit with a tree trunk. When he opened his eyes, he saw the demon standing over him, ready to give the final strike.

Suddenly, a stone came flying through the air, striking the back of the demon's helmet. Decimus turned around to see a small girl standing there defiantly. She was no bigger than the boy he about to kill. Decimus burst into laughter at the sight of her.

"Hey!" she called out. "Why don't you try knocking me down?"

Decimus laughed aloud once again. The boy and now this big-mouthed girl. He felt as if he'd stepped into some sort of comedy.

All eyes on the battlefield had been drawn to the two greatest warriors each nation had to offer. Bellus had stopped what he was doing as he caught sight of the red-headed warrior girl out on the open field. Even the Emperor, who had arrived on this throne, was next to Bellus, watching the scene unfold.

Delia drew her swords from her back. Decimus held onto his sword with his left hand and extended his wrist blade from his right arm. Decimus was determined to make this girl suffer.

Decimus quickly charged at Delia, intending to finish her off with one quick strike. However, Delia jumped into the air and expertly dodged his attack, following it up with a counter of her own. Decimus quickly realized how badly he'd understated the girl as she attacked so quickly, he was having a hard time seeing where the attacks were coming from.

Several times, Delia was able to get past his guard and strike Decimus on his armor. Unfortunately, his armor was too thick. Her blades only managed to cause scratches on the surface of the black armor Decimus wore. She knew she had to strike someplace weak, like near the ribs where the armor separated to allow for movement.

Decimus was breathing harder than in any battle he'd ever fought. The girl didn't seem human. She moved faster than it should've been possible. He only needed one opportunity to land a hit. Then he saw it.

As Delia continued to strike at Decimus, she realized she had lost her footing. She was too eager to strike a killing blow that she left herself open. She quickly covered her midsection. However, Decimus didn't go for her gut. He went lower and nicked her on the leg with his wrist blade. Delia backed off to recompose herself. The wound was superficial. Delia had suffered papercuts that were worse. She didn't understand it. Why would he forgo a lethal attack just to give her a tiny cut?

Decimus stood up from his kneeling position and began laughing.

What the hell was he so happy about? Delia thought.

As Delia prepared to strike again, she felt it. Her vision began to grow blurry. She looked down at her wound and saw the dark blue skin around the cut. She'd been poisoned!

Delia felt the world begin to spin. She finally understood the legend surrounding the demon. It was said the demon had defeated every champion of every nation. The demon was invincible and would never be defeated. The bastard didn't defeat anyone. He poisoned these champions and killed them while they were incapacitated.

Delia's heart began to pound in her chest. She collapsed onto her knees as the poison paralyzed her body. She suddenly felt something smash into her face, dropping her onto her back.

A heavy boot came crashing into her chest, knocking the wind out of her.

"Don't worry little girl." Decimus began. "The poison will not kill you. It will merely paralyze you for a time. Time enough for me to have my fun."

Decimus withdrew his wrist blade. He wanted to enjoy this moment. He reached down and grabbed Delia by the throat with his right hand. He lifted the girl up and drew closer to her face. He was so close, Delia could see his eyes through the slits of his helmet. She could smell the stink of his breath as he spoke.

"Your tongue will make a fine addition to my collection. I want you to know, I will use it to lick my balls before I hook it onto my belt." Decimus chuckled.

In one last act of defiance, Delia spit directly into the slit of Decimus' helmet. Decimus did not expect this. He turned his head and blinked several times as he tried to get the saliva out of his eye.

At that moment, Delia caught a glint of light out of the corner of her eye. Suddenly, she found herself falling backwards onto the ground. Looking up, Delia saw Breka, his sword in an upward angle. Decimus screamed as his arm had been severed, blood gushing out of the wound. The arm itself was still attached to Delia's throat. Delia quickly grabbed the arm and summoning her last bit of strength, extended the wrist blade and shoved it right into the weak spot of Decimus' armor.

Decimus groaned as his own blade, the one which was used to take the tongues of so many, cut into his gut and pierced the organs underneath. As Delia withdrew the blade, Decimus fell to his knees. Delia struggled to her feet and stood in front of the once invincible demon. Even on his knees, he was as tall as the young girl. Delia reached out and took the helmet off of Decimus' head. There was no demon staring back at her. It was just a man. A man who was in pain, with a look of fear in his eyes. It was a man who knew that the end was near. The same death he had dealt to so many people was now coming for him and it terrified him.

The Goddess

"You're no demon." Delia declared. "You're just a scared little man."

With that, Delia roared as she shoved the wrist blade, arm and all, down Decimus' throat. Decimus could not even scream. All he could do was gurgle as the blade pierced down his throat and into his wicked heart. Finally, Decimus fell backwards and collapsed on the ground dead.

There was silence across the battlefield. Both sides were in shock at what they had just witnessed. The Khalians couldn't believe the demon was finally dead. The Numerans couldn't believe their greatest champion had been killed by a woman and a boy.

Delia began to collapse again. However, she never hit the ground as Breka came to shoulder her. Breka put Delia on his back and piggybacked her as he began walking. He slowly trudged across the ground, as he made his way towards Andor's gate. The refugees he had been protecting had already made it to the city. The battle between Delia and Decimus had given them the time to get to safety. Now, it was up to him to do the same for Delia.

****

The entire Numeran camp was silent. Bellus couldn't believe what he had just witnessed. Even the Emperor was on his feet. Gradus was furious that his greatest warrior had been bested by a woman and feeble little boy.

The Numeran forces to the southwest were in complete disarray. After seeing their commander fall in battle, the will to fight had completely left them. Their will had taken a huge hit when the explosions began to rain down from the sky. Decimus' death was the nail in the coffin for them. They all began running for their lives, abandoning their posts.

Bellus knew he had to work fast to contain this situation. He couldn't afford to let the southwestern forces scatter. At the same time, the Khalians seemed to have some sort of weapon they weren't familiar with. It had shocked Bellus when the explosions first began. He didn't know what was happening. When he saw the smoke trails coming from a Khalian ship on the shore, Bellus realized this was something unexpected. He needed time to regroup his forces and reassess the situation.

"General! Send the men forward!" Gradus ordered.

Is he out of his mind? Bellus thought.

There was no way they could fight effectively at this moment. They needed to get things settled. They needed order.

"Your Majesty, we need to gain control of the southwestern forces." Bellus said.

"Attack the city, now!" Gradus yelled.

"The Khalians have a weapon we did not account for. We need to reassess the situation." Bellus argued.

"They are out of ammunition! Why do you think they stopped firing?" Gradus asked.

Bellus considered it for a moment. The Emperor could be right in this. The Khalians had not used their weapon in some time. They could be out of whatever explosions they had been using. Even if this were the case, they still needed to stop the men in the southwest from panicking and heading for the hills.

"Your Majesty, if we don't gain control of the forces to southwest, the Khalians could use that route to escape." Bellus explained.

The Emperor was impatient and bloodthirsty, but he wasn't a fool. He knew what Bellus was saying was true. Gradus wanted everyone in the city to suffer for what had just transpired on the field. He wasn't about to risk letting anyone get away.

"Very well, General. Do so quickly. My patience is at its limit." Gradus said.

Bellus breathed a sigh of relief and proceeded to issue orders. He sent messengers to the captains in the southwest. They needed to gain control of their men. Bellus was confident Andor would fall within the day. However, he also knew if the Khalians escaped, this war would never end.

****

Kara and her men disembarked from the Arita as soon as they had fired the last mortar round. Unfortunately, the weapon was useless now. Kara took solace in the fact that it did help to get the refugees into the city. It also provided a temporary relief to the Khalians fighting in the southwest. The Numeran army in the southwest was in a panic. Their officers were trying to regain order, but it would take time. Time for the Khalians to retreat back into the city.

As Kara and her company made their way to the Khalian forces, she was met by General Sulin. The general had separated the men into groups in order to make a retreat in an orderly fashion. He didn't want to risk retreating all at once, only to get ambushed. When Sulin saw Kara approaching, he extended his hand in welcome towards the princess.

"Welcome to the fight, princess." Sulin greeted.

The irony wasn't lost on Kara as she shook Sulin's hand. The man had always opposed her during the council meetings. However, Sulin knew if it wasn't for her arriving when she did, all his men would've been lost along with the innocent civilians trapped behind the Numeran lines.

"Was that the weapon you went after?" Sulin asked, referring to the mortar.

"Not exactly." Kara answered.

"Why didn't you bring it with you?"

Kara winced at the question before nervously saying, "Yeah, about that…"

Sulin stopped her and said, "Let me guess. You're out of whatever explosives you were using."

As Kara nodded yes, Sulin rubbed his head in frustration.

"At least it helped get the refugees into the city." Sulin said. "I guess it was worth something."

Gidor stepped up and said, "The Numerans may also realize we can't use the weapon any further. We should make a retreat before they send a force to finish us off."

"Agreed." Sulin said. "I've separated the men into three groups. While one group makes a retreat, the others will cover them. I'll remain with the last group and retreat with them."

"We'll stay with you, general." Kara said.

Sulin smiled in approval. He took Kara aside and said, "I know we haven't seen eye to eye on most issues, princess. However, I want you to know it's an honor to stand beside you in battle."

Kara just gave a smile back and patted the man on the shoulder.

"Begin the retreat!" Sulin ordered.

Sulin's lieutenant blew into his horn signaling the retreat. The first group of Khalians ran towards the city gate while the rest remained behind. For now, the Numerans still seemed to be in disarray but that could change momentarily once the Numerans caught on to what they were doing.

****

Bellus heard the Khalian signal horn sound and saw a a group of them run towards the gate. The Khalians were calling a retreat while the southwest was still in shambles.

Damn it! Bellus thought.

This was exactly what he was afraid of. Bellus thought quickly. He couldn't afford to let the defenders back inside.

Bellus grabbed a messenger and told him, "Get to the southwest. Tell the captains to press their forces forward."

The messenger rode off to deliver the message. Bellus turned to his lieutenant and said, "Signal the first two division to move forward and cut off the retreat."

The lieutenant immediately blew into his horn as four hundred men began to march forward at once. Bellus' plan was to surround the retreating Khalians and kill them on the open field. It was already too late to stop the first retreating group, but he could stop the rest if he acted quickly enough. While the forces in the southwest pressed forward, he would use the two divisions he'd just sent out from the main army to trap them.

The Khalians should then fall quickly as they would suffer attacks from both sides.

The first group had already made it to the gate. The second group was preparing to retreat.

Come on! Bellus thought.

The southwestern forces were now moving forward. They had engaged the Khalians and the two divisions Bellus had sent out were now in the act of taking positions. However, they were too late. The second group of Khalians fought through the Numerans before they could fully position themselves. Some of the Khalians fell but most got to the gate.

Goddamnit! Bellus cursed.

However, it wasn't a complete loss. The final group was completely cut off and surrounded. There was no way for them to get back. As Bellus looked on, he saw another sight to lift his spirits. Within the last group was a woman with red hair. It was the goddess. She was trapped with her men and surrounded by the enemy. At the very least, a thorn in the Numeran's side would be removed.

****

Breka was exhausted by the time he made it to the front of Andor's gates. He had carried Delia on his back from the southwest and arrived just in time to see the first group of Khalians retreating towards the walls. Breka felt like collapsing but he wasn't about to let Delia come to harm. He was going to carry her to safety even if it was the last thing he would do.

As the gates began to open for them, Delia woke up. She looked around and saw where she was. She also realized the small boy had carried her through the battlefield. She was both thankful and a bit embarrassed. She could never live it down to be carried inside in front of everyone. Not her, the greatest warrior in Khalia.

She tapped Breka on the shoulder and said, "I can walk."

Breka turned his head as he realized Delia had woken up. Despite his exhaustion, he was still a bit hesitant to put the wounded girl back down.

"Are you sure?" he asked.

"Yes. Thank you, Breka." Delia said.

Delia was still feeling the effects of the poison as her feet touched the ground. She wobbled a bit as Breka helped her maintain balance. Despite the poison still affecting the young girl, it was also wearing off. Delia wasn't feeling as bad as she had been on the battlefield when she fought Decimus.

Breka lent his shoulder to her as they both walked into the city. Everyone was on their feet cheering for their hero's return. She had proven her worth tenfold. No one could doubt the feat she had accomplished in front of her entire country. Nor would they deny her the due respect she deserved.

As Delia and Breka made their way up the wall, King Atlin ran over to his daughter and embraced her. He couldn't find the words to say. His embrace was enough. It told her how proud he was of the girl and how glad he was to see her again.

"Are you alright? Shouldn't you see a doctor?" Atlin asked.

Delia smiled as she always did and said, "I'm fine. We have a battle to finish."

Even Gallus came up to embrace the girl with a smile.

"I guess I trained you well." Gallus said with a laugh.

As the first group of retreating Khalians made it to the gate, everyone could see that a group from the main Numeran army had broken off and were attempting to surround the remaining Khalian forces still on the field. Atlin could see that Kara was still out there fighting alongside General Sulin. He wasn't going to lose any daughters today.

"Prepare a company of horsemen! Get my own horse ready!" Atlin shouted.

The men began to do as he ordered. Khalia didn't have many horses, which was why they lacked a cavalry. However, there was just enough to break the Numeran lines and get the rest of their people inside.

"Your Highness, you're going out there?" a captain asked.

"My daughter is out there!" Atlin shouted.

No one argued against the king. They knew he would do this regardless of any protest.

"Delia is in charge while I'm gone." Atlin declared.

"As you will, Your Highness." the captain said.

Before the battle against Decimus, putting Delia in charge would've been scoffed at by the men. However, no one challenged this decision now. Even poisoned, the girl was a better warrior than any of the men.

King Atlin and General Gallus climbed down the steps of the wall, heading for their horses. In all, they could only muster thirty horsemen, each of them volunteers and experienced riders. As Atlin mounted his saddle, he turned to his men and said, "Let's go get our people back!"

The gates opened again as the riders gave out a loud roar and rode out. They passed by the second group of retreating Khalians who managed to get away just before the Numeran formations closed the trap. That only left one group, the one where Kara was. As Atlin spurred his horse to move faster he could see the backs of the Numerans, clamoring to overwhelm the trapped group. They would be in for a terrible surprise when the horses collided with them.

****

Kara saw that the Numerans had surrounded their position. She and the others were completely cut off from retreat. The Numerans from the southwest continued to push forward while at the same time they were being attacked from the rear. Kara knew they wouldn't last long in this situation but there were no other options left.

"Damn it!" Sulin cursed as he took a spear to the shoulder.

Kara ran over, swinging her staff and cutting off the head of the Numeran aiming to finish Sulin off. She helped the man to his feet as he pulled the spear out of his body with a scream.

"Guess our time has come, princess." Sulin said.

Kara didn't want to admit it but Sulin was probably

right. At the very least, most of the men had made it to safety.

Just then, there was commotion from the rear. Kara looked back to see horses approaching. At first it looked like the Numerans had sent their cavalry to finish them off, but these horses were running the Numerans over. The Numerans to the rear scattered as they tried to avoid being trampled under the heavy hoofs of the animals. That's when she saw her father, leading the horsemen towards them.

"Fall back to the rear." Kara called out.

Sulin had seen the horses as well. This was their only opportunity to get out of this. He grabbed at his men and began pushing them towards the incoming cavalry.

"Kara, we have to go!" Aurin called out.

As Kara turned to leave, a Khalian soldier fell to the ground near her. The man scrambled for his sword which had landed on the ground beside him. Kara ran over and attempted to shield the man with her staff. The Numeran came down with his sword and cut straight through the wooden handle, splitting the staff into two pieces. Before Kara could regain herself, a young Numeran soldier, no older than a child, lunged out with his weapon. Kara felt the boy's sword stab into her gut.

"Kara!" Aurin called out as he attempted to fight his way towards her.

Kara held her hand to the wound, shocked at the sudden pain. Warm blood began flowing out, covering her hand. She looked up to see a surge of Numerans storming towards her. Her instinct was to raise her arm and guard herself from what was coming. However, her body wouldn't move. She could already feel the life draining out of her, the sounds of the battlefield softening.

She looked over at Aurin. She looked at the men who were scrambling to get onto the horses which had arrived to rescue them.

They'll be fine. They'll make it out of here. Kara thought.

That was all that mattered. Kara turned back just in time to see the face of the man who would deliver the killing blow. He plunged his sword directly into her chest, rupturing her heart. There was no pain this time. Kara fell to the ground, the world darkening around her. The only sound she heard was Aurin yelling out her name.

****

"Kara!" Aurin continued to yell.

The royal guard hacked away at whatever was in front of him. He no longer cared for anything other than getting to his friend. Blood covered his armor and his blade. The ground around him became littered with bodies, all lying on top of each other. Even so, he just couldn't get any closer.

Gidor and Sulin grabbed Aurin, trying to pull him towards the horses. Aurin tried to pull away from them. He didn't care if he died or not, he had to get to Kara. Aurin watched as Kara fell to the ground.

She's not dead. She can't be dead. Aurin kept saying to himself.

He only needed to get to her. If he could get to her, everything would be fine. They would get back to the city together.

"Damn it, Aurin! She's gone! We have to go!" Gidor shouted.

"Get off me! She's not gone!" Aurin insisted.

Aurin continued to fight against his comrades who were trying to restrain him. Even after a few other soldiers came to drag him back towards the city, Aurin kept freeing himself from their grasp.

Then, someone grabbed him by the shoulders firmly and turned him around. Aurin stopped fighting as he stared into the face of the man whom he failed. The same man who had the most right to be upset. It was King Atlin.

Staring into the face of Kara's father was too much for Aurin. A wave of shame, guilt, and failure hit the young man all at once. Aurin broke down and wept like a child. The king embraced the young man in his arms as he cried into his king's shoulder.

"It's alright, son. It's alright." Atlin said softly.

"I'm sorry. I failed. I failed her." Aurin wept.

Atlin pulled the man off and looked directly into his eyes.

"Until one of you should pass." Atlin said. "You protect her until one of you should pass. That was your oath. You have fulfilled it with honor. You have done your duty. You stood by her and protected her until her death. You have not failed."

Despite the words of the king, Aurin continued to weep. He couldn't help this feeling of guilt. Everything felt so empty. There was nothing left in him.

"Your Highness, we need to leave!" Sulin called out.

"Come." Atlin told Aurin.

The king literally dragged the man and pushed him up onto his horse. Aurin continued to weep as the king climbed on and spurred his horse towards the gate. The king himself could not help the tears that flowed down his face. He had just lost his beloved daughter. It was a feeling worse than any he'd felt in his life.

As Atlin wiped the tears away, he knew the battle was to continue. If he did not compose himself, many more sons and daughters would be lost this day. Atlin looked back one last time to see the Numerans surrounding the body of his precious little girl, celebrating the death of a woman so remarkable. He bid his daughter farewell and prayed that she find peace in death.

****

Bellus watched as the small Khalian cavalry exited the city walls to aid their comrades. He didn't have time to send his own cavalry or spearmen into action. He could do nothing as the horses broke the lines of his men and trampled those unlucky underfoot.

However, there was one small ounce of victory. The goddess was on the ground, lying in a pool of blood. Her royal guard was weeping as the king himself dragged the man away from the battlefield.

It was a small victory, but a victory, nonetheless. Bellus bowed his head in respect for the young woman. He had come to respect her bravery during this battle. She never abandoned her men or fled in the face of death. Bellus had even observed her risking her life to save a single fallen man. It was the reason she had fallen victim to the fatal blow. He wondered why she had fled during the Battle of Imbor when she had fought so bravely now. It didn't matter anymore. She had proven herself here and had died a warrior's death.

The battle wasn't over yet. It was time to storm the walls of Andor. This would not be easy. Bellus wondered how many other brave warriors awaited in the city, ready to follow the example of their fallen princess.

CHAPTER 10

Kara awoke to utter silence. It was an unnatural silence, one which should never exist. As she opened her eyes, she could hear nothing. Only the sounds of her shuffling movements filled the void. She was lying on a small circular platform, surrounded by clouds. It was as if the platform itself was flying through the air. Her armor and weapons were gone. She was dressed in an elegant gown, the likes of which she had never seen before. The royalty of Anaya would have been jealous of such material.

As Kara rose to her feet, a sense of peace washed over her. It was unlike any peace she had ever felt before. The peace she felt while on the cliffs of Khalia couldn't compare to what this felt like. Despite knowing where she had just come from, and the fact that the battle was still raging, everything felt right for some reason.

Kara went over to edge of the platform and brushed her foot against the clouds surrounding it. The clouds parted as her toes felt something solid. There was nothing there, but she could feel something hold her weight. It was as if someone had put a pane of glass down on the floor. Carefully, she took a step down. The clouds parted with each step she took. She wondered where she was until a voice rang out from the distance.

"Welcome back, my Lord."

Kara looked towards the voice and saw a man walking towards her. He was an old man, his face wrinkled with time. His skin was as black as tar, darker than the people of the southern nations. His white hair stood in stark contrast to his skin.

The man stepped towards her and extended his hand. She didn't know who this man was but for some reason, he seemed familiar. She took the man's hand as he led her to his side. They began walking along the clouds, side-by-side, towards no particular destination. There was nothing on the horizon except for more clouds.

"Where am I?" Kara finally asked.

"This is your kingdom." the man answered.

Kara chuckled under her breath. It wasn't much of a kingdom. There was nothing around. The place seemed completely desolate.

"Who are you?" Kara asked.

"I've gone by many names over time. Just as you have. Names are pretty things but meaningless. They come and go, much like the seasons you are familiar with." the man said.

"I'd still like to know what to call you." Kara insisted.

"Before you left, you would call me Jophiel."

"Left?"

"Before you left your kingdom."

Kara chuckled, this time aloud, and said, "It's not much of a kingdom. There's nothing here."

"This is only the entrance. Come, let me show you the wonders it holds."

Kara stopped walking and said, "Wait. I can't be here. There was a battle..."

"All irrelevant now." Jophiel interrupted. "The battle will go on without you."

"No, I have to go back." Kara insisted.

Jophiel sighed and said, "Your work is done, my Lord. Enjoy your peace."

It dawned on Kara that this was the second time Jophiel had to referred to her as "my Lord." She had to know the truth.

"Am I the reincarnation of Yalka?" Kara asked.

Jophiel smiled and said, "You have gone by many names, just as I. The people called you Yalka, now Kara. They have called you countless other things over time."

"So, it's true?" Kara asked almost rhetorically.

Jophiel didn't even answer this time. The smile on his

face said it all. The prophecy had been true, and she was the reincarnation of the Khalian god.

"Have I always been a woman?" Kara asked.

"You have been many things. Man, woman, other." Jophiel answered.

"Other?"

"Suffice it to say, in your true form, you are genderless. Right now, this female form is the one you are most comfortable with."

"Why was I born a woman? My life was miserable because of my gender."

"Because you chose to."

This was surprising to Kara. For her entire life, Kara had resented being born a woman. She felt if she had been born a man, she wouldn't have been persecuted and looked down on. Now, Jophiel was telling her it had been her choice all along.

Jophiel continued to explain, "You have always found empathy with those who were persecuted or oppressed. Whenever you would take the form of a mortal, you always chose to make it hard for yourself. Perhaps that is part of your charm, as they say."

This was a lot to take in for Kara. She always had doubts as to whether she truly was Yalka. Now, not only was this confirmed but the persecution she'd faced was due to her own decisions. She had asked for it.

"Come, my Lord." Jophiel began as he put his arm around Kara. "Your memories will return with time. Right now, let's get you someplace more relaxing. You often found solace near the cliffs of Khalia. They pale in comparison to the cliffs here. In fact, if you ask me, the cliffs in Khalia seemed quite ugly."

"I've always thought they were nice." Kara said.

Jophiel laughed and said, "You've always found optimism in everything."

"Wait." Kara said as she hesitated once again. "As nice as this all is, I can't leave my people there alone. They'll die if I leave them."

The Goddess

"Then they'll come here." Jophiel argued. "Death isn't the end. Your father, sister, royal guard, they will all join you here after death."

"Everyone?" Kara asked.

"Anyone whom you allow into the gates of your kingdom. Their own little slice of paradise, here with you." Jophiel explained.

It did sound nice. They could be away from it all. Numera could never harm them here.

"There's also someone here eager to meet you. Your mother." Jophiel said.

"My mother?" Kara asked in surprise.

Kara wondered what her mother was like. She'd never met the woman and this one statement was enough for Kara to consider staying.

"Wait, I wasn't here when my mother died." Kara began. "Who let her in?"

Jophiel chuckled as he answered, "It's complicated. You will understand all once you regain your memory and your powers."

"Powers?"

"The likes of which you can't even imagine right now."

"Why didn't I have powers..." Kara began to ask.

She didn't have to finish the question. She could answer it herself now. She didn't want the powers when she decided to be born in Khalia. The same way she chose to be born a woman.

Jophiel walked a few steps ahead of Kara. A door of light appeared in front of him. Kara had to momentarily cover her eyes at the brightness of it.

"Are you coming?" Jophiel asked.

Kara considered it for a moment. It was tempting. She wanted to meet the woman who had given her birth, the mother she never got a chance to know. She wanted to spend eternity in paradise and the thought that her family would join her was enticing.

"No." Kara answered.

Jophiel didn't seem too surprised by her answer. The way he was trying to convince her, Kara expected him to throw a fit or something. Instead he just gave a smile as if he expected it.

"You said my work was done, but it isn't." Kara began. "I'll admit, this is tempting. Life does seem irrelevant. It's so short. That doesn't mean you don't make the best of it while you're alive. Right now, the people in the living world are suffering because of evil. They deserve a chance to make their world into something more. They deserve to make the best of their lives, while it lasts. I can give that to them."

Jophiel smiled and said, "You don't remember it, but we have played this same scene countless times. Each time, you have decided to go back and help the people. You never change."

"Does that upset you?" Kara asked.

"On the contrary." Jophiel answered. "Part of your charm."

Jophiel turned towards the door as Kara called out, "Say hello to my mother for me. Tell her I love her."

Jophiel turned back with a smile and waved at Kara as he disappeared into the light of the door.

****

The Khalians looked on in horror from the walls as their princess' body was desecrated by the Numerans. Her armor was stripped, her broken weapon lay at the foot of the Emperor, and her nude body was nailed to a cross and raised up at the front of the army like a macabre banner. The Numerans cheered as the cross was raised, signifying their dominance over the woman and the Khalian people.

Aurin could not bear to look at the sight. As soon as he entered the city upon the king's horse, he dragged his feet to the nearest wall he could find and sat there, silent and unmoving. He could hear the cheers from the Numerans outside. He no longer cared for anything. He wished for some alcohol at the moment. One last cup of mead would be welcome before death.

Delia tried to hold her tears back and look brave in front

of her people. However, the sight of her sister was too much for her. The reality of Kara's death didn't hit the young girl immediately. From the walls, she had seen Kara fall in the field. She watched as Aurin fought against his own comrades as he tried desperately to get to Kara. She even watched as the Numerans surrounded Kara's lifeless corpse and began to cheer their victory. None of it made any sense to Delia. How could her sister be dead? Kara was the one who would save them. She was the reincarnation of Yalka. She couldn't be dead.

It wasn't until the Numerans began stripping Kara of her armor and nailing her body onto the cross did Delia finally come to realize the truth. Her sister was gone. She was dead and these animals were defiling her. As Delia stared at the bloody and beaten body of her sister, it was too much. Delia fell to her knees and began weeping harder than she'd ever done in her life. She couldn't remember the last time she cried. Whenever tears would come to her eyes, she would hold them back. She was always the strong one. Able to overcome anything with a smile and a sword. It was impossible to do now.

King Atlin couldn't help but keep looking at his daughter. It was bad enough that she had been killed but for her body to be desecrated was unforgivable. Kara had fought bravely and died as a warrior. She was the princess of a nation. Even an enemy should have respected that. The Numerans were worse than animals.

Gallus grabbed the king's shoulder as he tried to remove him from the walls. Atlin shouldn't have to see his daughter like this. Atlin refused to leave the sight as Gallus continually tried to convince him to make his exit. Finally, the king broke as well. He turned and began weeping as the others were. Gallus embraced his friend and held him tight. The king wept on his shoulder as Gallus tried to guide him down the steps of the walls.

The truth was, Gallus wanted to remove himself from the sight as well. Despite not being as close to Kara in recent years, he still helped to raise the girl from birth. He loved her and she was like a daughter to him. Just the thought of how she was now displayed, sickened Gallus. Coming down the wall, Gallus could see that he wasn't alone. Some of the people refused to even look at the sight of the princess' defilement. A few of those who had were vomiting from the sight.

There was no hope left in the city. Everyone was hoping that Kara could summon a miracle and save them from what was to come. Anger flared within Gallus. Weren't these the same people that had treated the princess like dirt her entire life? Now that the enemy was at the gates, they were hoping for a miracle? They were calling out to her to save them? As far as Gallus was concerned, these people were getting exactly what they deserved for treating Kara the way they had.

Some of the people in the city were falling upon their own swords. They would rather die now than suffer what awaited them when the Numerans came. Nobody tried to stop them. Everyone knew the end was inevitable. If someone chose to end their life the way they wanted, it was their choice. Some who witnessed these mass suicides began to wonder if they should follow. Perhaps these people had the best idea. End the suffering now rather than live a moment longer with this dread.

The one snake that was taking advantage of all this was Tula. He was preaching doom and hellfire to the masses as he always did. However, this time he was right. There was nobody that could deny that Yalka had forsaken them.

"Yalka punishes us!" Tula preached. "This was the fault of that she-devil out on the field. This was the fault of your leaders for allowing her to live. If you had heeded my words when that whore was born, you would have been spared the wrath of Yalka."

Gallus considered going over and killing the man. Who would care at this point? The only reason Gallus didn't was because he knew that Tula was in for suffering once the Numerans arrived. He was in the same sinking boat they were. Did the fool really think that because he was a priest the Numerans would spare him? They'd probably make an example of him and cause him to suffer longer. It was a deserved fate for such a vile individual.

The others seemed to know it as well. Despite Tula's insistence that they pray for Yalka's mercy, no one was paying attention to the man. The only priest that was doing anything worthwhile was Reverend Miru. Instead of preaching to the people, the man was going around asking if they needed anything. Of course, most people just wanted to be left alone to face death on their own terms. However, he managed to offer what little comfort he could to the few who asked for it.

There were still a few who asked for prayer. However, Miru wasn't praying for deliverance or a miracle. He was praying that they would have the courage to face death when it came. It was a comforting form of realism. It was the acceptance of what was to come rather than living in a fantasy.

Gallus was never a very religious man himself. However, when a soldier near Miru asked for prayer, Gallus closed his eyes and prayed along with the two.

"Yalka." Miru began. "We do not know whether you hear us or not. We would like to believe that you do and have not forgotten us. All we ask is for courage when the time comes. Courage to face the enemy and to face death when it comes. In death, we ask that you remember your faithful. Please, open the gates of your kingdom to your people. Let us leave this world with our heads held high and know that we will spend eternity with you."

Gallus opened his eyes wondering when the last time he prayed was. Gallus was almost a teenager when his mother immigrated to Khalia. He never adhered to the Khalian religion. He only followed along because it was what everyone else was doing. He realized he had never truly prayed. That was until this very moment. He truly hoped that Yalka was real and that the god was hearing these prayers.

****

Bellus watched as the men raised the cross with the princess' body ahead of the army. They cheered, almost as if their victory was assured. For the most part, it was. The symbol of hope that kept the Khalians fighting was now dead and defiled in front of them. This was a huge hit to the morale of the Khalians. Bellus doubted there would be many left in the city who still had the will to fight.

When the Emperor had ordered the princess stripped and nailed to the cross, Bellus had almost spoken out against it. The girl was royalty. She had also fought bravely. She deserved some form of a decent burial at the very least. It hadn't surprised Bellus that the Emperor would do this. He'd ordered something similar in Imbor when the king fell. The Emperor had ordered the man's body decapitated, his head hung on a post for all the defenders to see. At least that was just his head. Bellus had ordered the men to bury the king's body along with his men.

Even now, as Bellus stood next to the Emperor's throne, he tried to think of ways to remove the gruesome cross which acted as a banner. He had success earlier in convincing the Emperor to delay the advance of the troops. Perhaps he could speak to the Emperor's better nature here. That is, if the man had a "better nature" which Bellus doubted.

"Your Majesty, perhaps we should bury the girl before commencing the final attack." Bellus suggested.

"Are you blind, General? The girl will be at the head of the army. A symbol of our victory over her and the Khalian people." Gradus said.

"Your Majesty, this may convince the Khalians to resist further. It may galvanize them to try to avenge their fallen princess."

This was a complete lie and Bellus knew it wouldn't convince the Emperor. The Khalians were completely demoralized by this sight. Bellus had even caught sight of Delia collapse onto her knees at the sight of her sister. The brave warrior woman, the same one who had defeated Decimus, was reduced to tears at the sight of her sister. Bellus had never truly felt empathy with his enemies until now.

Bellus could only imagine how he would be feeling if Nola were up on the cross. The very thought made him sick to his stomach. Would he break down in tears in front of all his men? He imagined it was something he wouldn't be able to control. He could try to hold the tears back. He could try to get to his tent before being hit with the feelings of despair. He surmised that he wouldn't be able to make it though. Just as Delia wasn't able control herself now. He couldn't fully understand what she was going through, not without having gone through it himself, but he could imagine.

"Enough, General!" Gradus bellowed. "I grow tired of your weakness. Thank whatever gods you pray to that this will be your final battle. I cannot bear to have such weakness in my presence any further."

In the past, Bellus would've been offended by such words. He would've tried to prove himself and show the Emperor that he wasn't weak. However, Bellus finally understood the truth. There was no weakness in caring for others. There was value in life, whether you were royalty or a slave. It was a lesson Nola had taught him. If Gradus felt that strength came from cruelty, then so be it. That was something Bellus felt no intention of being a part of any longer.

"Sound the assault!" Gradus ordered.

Bellus looked to his lieutenant and gave him a nod. The lieutenant blew into his horn, signaling all the men forward. Bellus looked over to Gradus, sitting on his throne. He couldn't see the Emperor's face through the thick helmet he wore, but Gradus imagined the man was smiling. This was the day Gradus had been waiting for. The day Emperor Gradus of Numera conquered the world and proclaimed his dominance over all.

The Numeran army continued to march, eager to lay waste to the city before them. Before they had made it halfway to the gate, something unexpected happened. A bright light engulfed the battlefield, blinding everyone. A silence enveloped the surroundings. The army ceased to march as the men sought to understand what was happening. Bellus had to blink several times in order to regain his sight.

It took a moment for everyone to realize where the light was coming from. It was coming from the cross, from the body of the fallen princess. Her body floated off the cross but remained in the air. The wounds on her body healed instantly before the eyes of the men. Then she suddenly awoke, taking a deep breath and raising her head. Her body was no longer nude but covered in the most brilliant white armor anyone had laid their eyes on. The broken staff which lay at the Emperor's feet flew into the princess' hands, reassembling itself. However, it was no longer a wooden staff as it was before. Now, the blades on either end were adorned with jewels. Blue cursive writing of an unfamiliar language flowed through the blades as if enchanted by magic runes. The handle itself was a pure gold that blinded those who looked upon it for too long.

She floated there in the air for several seconds, then turned towards the Numeran army. No one could deny the magnificence of the being that hovered over them. She shined more brightly than the sun. Her eyes glowed white as they looked down upon the encroaching army. There was no fear in the eyes of the men, only bewilderment. Their minds could not fully comprehend what they were looking at. Fear had not caught up to them yet.

****

As the Khalians wept in the city, they were also blinded by the sudden brilliant light, the same as the Numerans. Many had turned away from the walls, unable to look upon the princess' battered body or the impending doom coming for them. However, once the light passed, they all ran to see what was happening outside the gates.

Delia, who had shed more tears in the past few minutes than in her entire lifetime, saw the light radiating from her sister's corpse. She saw as her sister floated off the cross, her body instantly healing itself. She saw the armor that appeared to cover her nakedness, the divine weapon reassembling in her hand. She had always believed in her sister. Hope had been gone momentarily but now it was back again.

I knew you wouldn't abandon us. Delia cried.

Delia's tears turned to those of joy. Not just at the return of hope, but at the return of her sister. She was alive and stronger than ever. Her sister had conquered death itself and was now poised to protect them from this monstrosity before them. The prophecy was true.

Just like the Numerans, the Khalians did not know what to think. Despite the prophecy, they had always treated Kara as a curse. Most of the people had come to accept their demise. They didn't expect the prophecy to be true and certainly didn't expect it to come to fruition like this. Many still did not know whether Kara would save them or condemn them.

Not even King Atlin or General Gallus knew what to think. Their first thought was that this could just be another cruel ploy by the Numerans. One last mockery against the beliefs of the Khalian people. However, even they could not deny the majestic aura that surrounded Kara. Just looking at her told the truth. It filled everyone with strength and warmth just to see her figure in the sky.

As she floated there, it dawned on them all. The prophecy said that she would be a protector, guide, and commander. She had been all these things in her life. She was to bring a new era for Khalia and lead it to greatness. There was no longer any doubt in the hearts of the Khalian people. Kara was their goddess.

****

Bellus did not know what to think. They had always called the princess "goddess." It was meant to be an insult, a mockery of the Khalian's beliefs. Now, they were witnessing the truth of it. The girl truly was a goddess. She had come back from the dead, more beautiful than ever. She radiated strength and hope for the people of Khalia. Just looking at her now, Bellus knew she was of the divine. There could be no denying it.

Bellus turned to the Emperor, hoping he had some idea of what to do. Instead, even the Emperor was on his feet, his head raised towards the image of the goddess standing in front of them. Bellus didn't know what was going through the man's mind but if he was the Emperor, the only thing going through his mind would be fear. The goddess looked as if her wrath were radiating from her body. Bellus didn't want to be the target of that wrath.

The goddess finally spoke, her voice echoed across the battlefield. It didn't matter if you were right next to her or all the way at the back, near the main camp. All could hear her words as if she were standing right next to you. It was as if the goddess was speaking with multiple voices at once, both male and female. Yet, her words came as one. It was one person speaking, one god.

"I am Kara, reincarnation of Yalka, goddess of the people of Khalia!" Kara declared. "You have threatened those that I love and brought suffering unto the world. Lay down your arms and surrender or suffer my wrath!"

The Numerans were finally filled with terror at the realization of what they were seeing and hearing. They could not fight against a goddess. This battle was beyond them now.

"General!" Gradus bellowed. "Fire a volley of arrows! Knock that bitch out of the sky!"

Is he insane? Bellus wondered.

Just how the Emperor thought they could fight against this was beyond Bellus' understanding. They should be surrendering, doing exactly what the goddess demanded, not trying to engage this divine being.

When Gradus realized his General's hesitation, he turned directly to the lieutenant with the signal horn and shouted, "Fire the arrows!"

The lieutenant snapped out of his bewilderment as the Emperor shouted at him. He blew into his signal horn but most of the archers were reluctant to fire, lest they anger the goddess. However, some of them heeded the call for arrows and drew

The Goddess

back their bows. There was no order to their attack. They fired at will hoping the goddess was not as powerful as she looked.

About a dozen arrows flew through the air. Some of the arrows missed entirely, fired from hands too shaky to hold their bows steady. The ones that managed to find their target were all but ineffective. The heads of the arrows broke off harmlessly as they struck the goddess. This was enough of a response for Kara.

Before anyone could even blink, Kara slammed into the ground with a devastating force unlike anything the Numerans could have imagined. Dozens of men around her flew into the air. Some of them crashed into their comrades while others were dead before they even hit the ground. Kara immediately started swinging her staff. With each swipe, dozens of men flew into the air. Blood and body parts began raining down onto the panicked Numeran forces.

None of the Numerans had the will to fight anymore. Those on the frontlines abandoned their weapons and began running back towards the main camp. There was no one brave or foolish enough to challenge the goddess or go towards her. The entire army was focused on thing – fleeing.

"Lieutenant!" Bellus called out. "Signal a retreat! Full retreat!"

"No!" Gradus shouted. "Signal the men forward. Prepare the archers and shoot any who retreat! They are deserters and will be executed!"

Bellus stared at the man as if he had gone completely mad. Was he blind to what was going on?

"Emperor, the men are helpless! We cannot fight against this!" Bellus argued.

"Do as I say!" Gradus ordered.

Bellus looked over at the lieutenant. He had been here before, months ago when Gradus ordered the men forward into Anayan arrows. The lieutenant had the same look on his face as back then. It was the look of a man begging him not to send the men into certain death. Bellus had followed Gradus' orders back then and it haunted his dreams since. He was not about to make the same mistake again.

"No!" Bellus said.

Gradus looked at his general. Despite the helmet on the Emperor's head, Bellus could tell that the man was shocked. No one had ever refused his orders. Gradus had probably never even heard the words "no" since he came into power.

"Our men are dying!" Bellus began. "I will not let you waste their lives any longer."

Bellus turned to his lieutenant again. The man had a different look on his face now. One that said he was proud of his general and was honored to follow a man who cared for the lives of those who served under him.

"Call a retreat, lieutenant." Bellus ordered.

It was the last words out of Bellus' mouth. Gradus had stepped off this throne, drawn his sword, and severed the man's head with a single swing. The lieutenant stood there in shock at seeing his beloved general's head just inches from his feet.

"Enough of this!" Gradus bellowed. "I will handle this myself!

Gradus walked onto the battlefield as his men scrambled to escape the wrath of the goddess. Soon, he and the goddess were the only ones on the open field. The eyes of the world seemed to be upon them.

Emperor Gradus was still intimidating to look at. His armor was unlike anything in the world. His large sword was sharp and glowing. There was blue writing shining from it, not unlike that of Kara's blades. As the two stared each other down, the Emperor pointed his sword at Kara. Suddenly, a bolt of lighting shot out from the sword and hit Kara square in the chest. Kara flew through the air, almost all the way to Andor's gates. Kara was able to flip in the air and land on her feet, but she also looked surprised. She was clearly not expecting such an attack.

Gradus began to laugh at Kara's stunned expression and said, "My weapons were created to fell gods. I fear no one, not even you. My destiny is to rule this world and you will not stand in my way."

The Goddess

With that, Gradus once again extended his sword. However, Kara was ready for it this time. With lightning speed, she dodged the next shot. Gradus continued to fire his weapon at Kara. She moved too quickly for him. Kara moved from one spot to another in the blink of an eye. It was impossible to track her movements. Gradus began to panic as the girl got closer and closer. He began to shoot at anything on the field, whether Kara was near it or not.

Finally, Kara was right on top of him. She jumped into the air and raised her staff over her head. Gradus instinctively raised his sword to block the incoming blow. A noise like an explosion filled the air as the two made contact. Gradus was thrown back several yards. He crashed into the ground, his sword coming to a rest a few feet away from him.

Gradus slowly got to his feet. The front of his armor had a large slash in it. Fire and sparks began to fly from the damaged area. It was if the man was a machine rather than human. He stumbled over to his sword. As he picked it up, the sword began to spark as well. Kara was once again shocked that the man had survived her hit. The others in the Numeran army were killed by the dozen with a simple swipe of Kara's weapon. Yet, Gradus had somehow survived a powerful hit from Kara. Not only that but the man was actually walking and ready to fight again.

Gradus pointed the weapon again at Kara. He tried to fire a bolt of lightning, but the weapon only sparked. It was clear the weapon had been damaged by Kara's blow. Gradus angrily threw the sword on the ground.

"Fuck the sword! I don't need it!" Gradus screamed as he charged at Kara.

Kara almost pitied the man as he desperately came charging at her. As Gradus got close, she took a quick swipe at him. Once again, Gradus was thrown back. This time, Gradus struggled to get back up. The armor he wore was beginning to fall apart in places. It continued to spark as the sword did, indicating a significant amount of damage. Blood fell onto the ground at Gradus' feet. He was not a machine but a man after all.

The light surrounding Kara began to radiate even more. Once again, the goddess spoke and filled the silent battlefield with the fierce echo of her voice.

"Emperor Gradus." Kara began. "You have committed unspeakable acts of evil against the people of this world. For this, your punishment is clear."

A bright fiery light shot out from Kara and swirled around as if alive. It gained speed and size as it made its way straight for Gradus. As the Emperor stood there, fear gripped his heart for the first time in years. He knew there was no escaping this. Gradus raised his arms to protect himself as the light got closer. At the same time, he knew it was futile. He had lost. His campaign was over and so was his life.

As the light blasted into Gradus, the entire battlefield was engulfed in light and dust. Everyone coughed and blinked as sand and dust covered their faces. Soon, the dust began to settle, and everyone looked out to see the end result. Gradus stood there but everyone knew he was dead. Those who had doubts only had to look at the large gaping hole in his chest. It was so large, you could literally see the Numerans on the other side of his body through it.

Gradus' corpse fell to its knees, then finally slumped face first onto the ground. It was unclear if his spirit had left him long ago or if he was still grasping to stay in the world as he fell. It didn't matter. What mattered was that the Emperor of Numera was dead.

Kara walked slowly over to the Numeran army. They had just seen their Emperor killed and their general was no longer there to command them. Kara stared at them with her white glowing eyes, challenging any to step forward. A captain finally came forward, but instead of attacking, he dropped his weapon at her feet and knelt on the ground in surrender. A cascade began as each Numeran did the same as the captain. The silent battlefield began to be filled with the sounds of metal hitting the ground as every single Numeran disarmed and surrendered to the goddess.

The Goddess

The white light in Kara's eyes disappeared, replaced by her normal green. For the first time since her return to life, Kara's lips curled into a smile. The battle was over. The entire war was over. The Numerans had capitulated and Khalia had been spared destruction. Kara's people had been saved.

****

The gates of Andor opened for their goddess. Kara walked into the city which was filled with silence. There were no cheers or celebrations. Everyone took a knee of reverence at the presence of their savior and their deity. They felt unworthy to look upon her. They had treated her as an outcast for her entire life. Despite that, she had always cared for them and loved them. In their most desperate hour, she had even conquered death in order to save them.

Even King Atlin and Delia didn't know what to say or do. They stood in front of her, not knowing whether to approach her or bow before her. Kara just chuckled as she went over and embraced her family.

"It's me." Kara confirmed. "Same as always."

Kara's voice was no longer that of when she was on the battlefield. She had returned to the single feminine voice she had always had.

"Well, not really the same." Delia joked as she wiped away her tears.

Kara looked into her sister's face and said, "What's this? The brave and courageous Delia in tears? What's the world coming to."

"The world's changing." Atlin said he embraced his eldest tightly.

The lovely moment was broken at the sound of a grating voice. Archbishop Tula was being the snake he'd always been, looking for an opportunity to turn these events to his advantage.

"As I said." Tula began. "Kara is the savior of Khalia. I told you all that if you have faith, you will be delivered. Give thanks to Yalka that you did not harm this child when she was born."

The people glared at the priest, knowing that it was he who had almost damned them. Tula had been leading them falsely for years and none of this was lost on them. They would have beat and killed the man had the goddess not been standing there.

In that instant, there was one man who wasn't afraid to act. He did what everyone wanted to. Personally, he had wanted to do this since he'd met Tula. Aurin ran up and punched Tula in the face, laying the priest flat on his back. Tula crawled across the ground at the sudden assault. He wiped the blood from his face as he lay there.

"You dare?" Tula began. "I am the archbishop of Yalka. I am the representative of our god. I am..."

Kara interrupted the man as she went over and grabbed him by the throat. She easily lifted the man into the air as her eyes became white again in rage. Everyone stepped back away from her, fearing the wrath of the goddess. Even Aurin and Delia stepped back, wondering what Kara would do to Tula. The display she had put on when she killed Gradus was still fresh in everyone's minds.

"You speak for no one but yourself!" Kara declared in anger.

Instead of killing Tula, as he rightfully deserved, Kara threw him back onto the ground. Kara calmed herself and the light of her wrath ceased from her body. She turned to the people, seeing the fear in their eyes.

"A man like this should never be in charge of the church." Kara began. "This snake has ruined the good name of Yalka. He has ruined my name. A true priest should be merciful and understanding."

Kara spotted Reverend Miru standing amongst the crowd with a smile on his face. Kara smiled back and looked at him with love in her eyes as she continued, "A true priest, is someone who gives comfort to the least when they need it. Someone who acts as a friend, even when the rest of the world hates you."

Kara turned back to the rest of the people and said, "Do not forget these words when you choose a new archbishop."

A new beginning had arrived. There was still much work to be done, but it was a new era for Khalia. It was a new era for the world. King Atlin had been right when he said the world was changing. It was time for Khalia to take its place in it.

EPILOGUE

Six months since wars end...

Kara closed her eyes and breathed in the clear air of the Khalian cliffs. Summer had arrived but there was still a bit of snow on the ground. There was always snow in Khalia. The waves crashed onto the shore, but another sound was now vibrant in the air. Kara looked below the cliffs to see children playing by the shoreline. They ran around and even used the remains of the Arita as their playground. To think that a weapon of war was now being used for the joy and happiness of children brought a smile to Kara's lips. She was sure her mother would approve. The woman's namesake was no longer attached to an object meant for war.

Jophiel had told her that the cliffs of Khalia paled in comparison to what awaited her when she returned to her kingdom. Kara looked forward to it. She would miss the home she had grown up in. However, all things changed with time. Whether it was tradition, a nation, or people, nothing was a constant in this world. It's always sad when things change, and the past is left behind. However, things could always end up better. Sometimes, change is something to be embraced, not avoided.

As Kara stroked the mane of her horse, she heard the gallop of another rider coming up beside her. She didn't have to turn to know who it was. Delia always seemed to spur her horse a certain unique way.

"They're ready for us." Delia said as she stopped next to Kara.

Kara looked at her sister with a smile. The girl was now officially the heir and princess to the Khalian throne. The announcement had been met with a few discontented voices. However, the goddess herself approved of the decision and the majority of the Khalian people had not forgotten what the girl did during the war. She was instrumental in saving the country. These reasons were vindication enough to silence the critics.

"How does it feel it know you're going to be queen one day?" Kara asked.

Delia chuckled and said, "They call me *orphan princess*."

The term was meant to be an insult by those who opposed the succession, the same way Kara used to be called goddess. However, Kara now embraced the name. She was sure Delia would make an excellent queen one day.

"You'll have to choose a royal guard." Kara said.

"Ugh, don't remind me." Delia groaned. "Everyone's been on me about that since the announcement."

"At least they're letting you choose."

The war had interrupted the military training all Khalian males had to go through. Those few who survived the war weren't considered to be royal guard material in the eyes of the council. Therefore, King Atlin proposed that Delia should be allowed to choose her own royal guard when she felt the time was right. Nobody opposed the idea. Delia was capable of protecting herself, as she'd proven during the war. No matter who she chose, she would be a better warrior anyway.

"Are you ready?" Delia asked.

Kara took one last breath and said, "Let's go."

As the girl's turned their horses around, they caught sight of Aurin a few yards away. The man was leaning forward on his horse, a smile on his face. He always seemed to be smiling these days. It was far different from before when he always looked so serious.

"He is aware that he no longer has to protect you, right?" Delia asked rhetorically.

"As long as you're here in this world, my duty doesn't end. His words." Kara answered.

The girls chuckled as they rode towards Aurin, and together, headed for the city.

****

The Numeran army camp was still present in front of Andor. They were packing up to leave but not before today's meeting. It had taken six months for everything to be set and agreed upon. As the three friends headed towards Andor, Kara could see smiling faces within the Numeran camp. The men were happy to be going back home as well.

The gates of Andor remained open all year long now. Anyone was free to come and go as they pleased. Even men from the Numeran army camp were permitted to come and do business with the merchants or have a drink at a tavern. There was still much tension between the Numerans and Khalians. Several fights had broken out when the Numerans were first permitted into the city. This was expected but King Atlin believed the healing process had to begin. Over the past few weeks, the animosity seemed to have calmed down. Everyone was trying to rebuild their lives and pursue their happiness.

Everyone was present as the three friends made their way into the royal palace. People were still walking around and greeting one another, conservation filled the spacious room of the throne room. Archbishop Miru bowed and greeted the three as they walked in. Miru had been voted unanimously as the new Archbishop of Khalia. In his mercy, Miru even offered Tula a position in a church, somewhere quiet where he couldn't cause any trouble. Instead, Tula opted for self-exile. Tula's reputation had been ruined. He decided to leave Khalia and spew his poison elsewhere rather than live amongst people that despised him.

King Atlin stood up from his throne as his daughters walked in. He embraced each of them as well as Aurin before sitting back in his seat.

"Are you nervous." Atlin asked Delia.

The new princess had been tasked with being the mediator for this meeting. It was Delia's first test to show everyone that she could one day take the throne and be a great leader. The agreement that was to be presented was drawn up by Delia and several different representatives of the nations of the world. As soon as the war ended, riders were sent out to every nation in order to spread the news. Khalia had done the impossible and peace had returned to the world. Even so, it took time to gather everyone. Some felt that this was some Numeran trick to get those in hiding out into the open. However, as time went by, it was obvious to everyone that Numera was no longer the authority it was under Emperor Gradus. People began to come back to their homes and rebuild what had been lost.

People had heard about how the goddess, Kara, had stopped the Khalians. Some doubted the fantastical story, yet others could not fathom how a small nation like Khalia could have stopped the Numerans if this were not true. Either way, Khalia gained influence in the world. They were no longer considered a small backwards people. They were the saviors of the world and many of the other nations assumed they would take a leadership role as the world moved forward.

It had taken time for these other nations to choose who would represent them. Many of their leaders had been killed during the war. Once these new leaders were selected, they were sent to Khalia to make this peace official. This was the purpose of the meeting today.

Delia let out a loud breath and said, "I'm alright. I've always been a warrior, not a politician."

"You'll have to be both when you become queen." Kara said with a smile.

Delia rolled her eyes and said, "Stop reminding me."

Atlin caressed Delia's cheek. The girl held her father's hand and closed her eyes, delighting in the affectionate touch of a parent. Kara smiled at the irony. A few months ago, Delia would have recoiled at such shows of emotion. It was said that children grew to miss these things as they got older. They longed for their parents' touch, the more infrequent they became. This war definitely forced many people to get older, Delia included.

The king clapped his hands, signaling the start of the meeting. The representatives took their seats at the table in front of them. Numera had elected a new Emperor from the surviving officers in the camp. This man was Emperor Theodus. He was a captain who had served under Bellus since the Anayan campaign. The Numerans sat at the far end of the table, across from the king. The others at the table were representatives from Anaya, Sarina, the Southern Alliance, and several other nations the Khalians had only heard tales about or didn't even know existed.

Delia began the meeting by saying, "Thank you to everyone for coming. We all know why we're here. Now that the war is over, we must discuss the future and agree upon a lasting peace treaty."

Delia felt so awkward doing this. She never asked to be queen or even the princess. She had hoped Kara would handle this, but her sister was adamant in staying out of it. Kara had not even participated in drafting the agreement itself, leaving it up to Delia and the representatives to handle.

"Numera will be at the center of this agreement." Delia continued. "I think it should be obvious to everyone as to why."

Theodus looked down at the table when this was said. He had been expecting this day for the past six months. His side had basically lost the war. Now, it was up to the victors to state the terms.

Delia continued, "First, Numera will relinquish all captured territories to the people they seized land from. Numera will go back to their national borders from before the war began. National lines will be redrawn according to what they were from before the war. This applies to all nations."

Delia looked around wondering if there were any objections. She expected Numera to say something, but this was the least of the demands they would make. She was glad the meeting was off to a good start.

"Second, Numera will forever relinquish any claims outside of their national borders. Third, the Numeran army will be disbanded."

This third condition led to some disgruntled sounds from the Numerans. Their entire nation was built around the military. To disband it would mean hundreds of men who would now be scattered to the winds. Theodus calmly put his hand up to calm his own people.

"What if we're attacked?" Theodus asked. "I'm sure there are many who would feel some retaliation against Numera would be a good idea."

"You will be allowed an army." Delia said. "It will be limited. Your army will never surpass the numbers of the Khalian and Anayan forces combined. We *will* enforce this. If you are attacked, the Khalian and Anayans will come to your aid. Your sovereignty will be respected and defended."

This led to some grumbling from the others. However, everyone had agreed to this beforehand. It was written into the document itself.

"Our army has thousands of men." Theodus argued. "Many have no particular skills other than being soldiers. Where are we to put them all?"

This time, Delia impatiently stared down the new Emperor.

"Find something." Delia demanded.

The fire in Delia's eyes was not lost to anyone in the meeting. Even Theodus backed down after seeing the young girl's reaction. Even if the goddess were not present, Theodus dared not challenge Delia at the moment.

Delia continued, "Fourth, Numera will return all national treasures taken from their rightful owners."

Nobody argued this but Kara raised her hand. Everyone was surprised the goddess was intervening. She had not shown much interest in involving herself with political affairs up to this point. Delia nodded at Kara, wondering what her sister wanted to say.

"I just have a quick suggestion." Kara began. "Numera has acquired a substantial amount of riches during their conquests.

Is that true?"

Theodus nodded wondering if they were to give up these riches as well.

"Then I suggest you use that to reinvigorate your economy, Emperor." Kara said. "Use that wealth to invest in things that will make your economy self-sufficient. That way, all the men who will be affected by the disbandment of your army will have work after this war."

No one could argue the logic behind this suggestion. In fact, Theodus felt that this was a good idea. The coffers would take a huge hit, but their nation would not be in shambles.

"Thank you for the suggestion, your grace. I assume the other leaders present will not object to Numera using its wealth in such a way?" Theodus asked.

No one objected although some felt Numera should have returned the stolen wealth as well.

Delia continued, "Finally, slavery will be abolished, worldwide."

This final condition led to an uproar from the Numerans. Even Theodus stood up and slammed his fist against the table.

"This is ridiculous!" Theodus screamed. "We freed the slaves in the main army camp as you demanded. Now you want to free them in our entire nation as well?"

"Slavery will be abolished!" Delia yelled back.

This led to a chorus of arguments between the Numerans and the rest of the people in the room. When it became clear that order was being lost, King Atlin stood up and bellowed out, "Silence!"

The room immediately settled. No one dared to disrespect the Khalian king in his own throne room. King Atlin sat down as Theodus calmed himself. He took a deep breath before arguing his case.

"Our entire nation runs on slavery. We have had slavery since the founding of our nation. We cannot operate without it."

"Well then, I guess that's alright." Delia said sarcastically.

The Goddess

Everyone looked at Delia wondering if she was being serious. Delia frowned as she looked at the people around the room.

Did these people not know what sarcasm was? Delia thought.

"Slavery must be abolished!" Delia screamed. "This is not an option!"

Once again, the room devolved into a screaming contest. Kara stood up from her seat and the room settled down. They dared not offend the king but even more so, the goddess.

"We will help you rebuild your nation, without slaves." Kara calmly told the Numerans.

"What?" Delia almost screamed as she turned to Kara.

"This is preposterous!" one of the Anayan representatives shouted.

"They should be paying us reparations!" a Sarinan representative added.

Even reverend Miru looked towards Kara as if she'd lost her mind.

Kara held her hand up to settle everyone. No one had dared challenge anything the goddess had to say until now. For the past six months, whatever Kara said, the people did. There would sometimes be some grumbling as they did it, but they did not want to offend the goddess and suffer her wrath. This time, the goddess was proposing that they aid the aggressors. It was too much for them to accept.

"Here me out." Kara calmly said to everyone. "We are here to build a better world. One in which we will all stand united, even with Numera. If we leave Numera in shambles, someone like Gradus will rise again. Perhaps someone even worse next time. The only way our world gets better is with a stable Numera. We must rebuild Numera, just as much as we rebuild our own nations."

Nobody liked what the goddess was saying but it also rang true in the hearts of many. The reason Gradus rose to power in the first place was because of the state Numera was in. If that could be prevented for future generations, they had to accept what Kara was saying.

Delia was one of those people who hated the idea. However, she also knew that Kara was right. She gritted her teeth and said, "Very well. Are there any objections?"

Delia knew there had to be objections running in the hearts of many, including herself. However, no one wanted to see another Gradus. Therefore, everyone held their tongues.

Seeing that all was silent, Delia placed the agreement onto the table and was the first to sign her name on it. She passed it to her father who signed it as well. The agreement was passed around until every representative signed the document. It finally came to Emperor Theodus. It was clear the Emperor was not happy with many of the conditions. However, he also wanted the best for his nation and right now, this was for the best. The world was changing and Numera had to change with it.

As Theodus signed his name onto the agreement, applause rang out from the people present. The lasting peace was official. There were smiles all around as the war was officially over. Hands were shaken, albeit reluctantly with the Numerans.

When Delia and Theodus finally shook hands, the man smiled at the young girl and said, "You will make a remarkable queen one day, fierce and strong. Be well, princess."

Theodus bowed before leaving the royal palace. Delia didn't know how to feel. She had looked upon the Numerans as her enemy for so long. Yet, she was flattered by the compliment. For the first time, Delia felt confident that she could be a good leader for her people.

****

Seven months since wars end...

Kara looked upon the fields of Imbor. It was breathtaking to look upon it now. The flowers bloomed as the butterflies floated around them. There were so many vibrant colors, all different in their shapes and appearances. The last time Kara had been on this exact same hill, the Numerans were swarming

The Goddess

around the area.

"You ready to go in?" Aurin asked.

Kara shook her head yes. She was lost for words at the beauty that had returned to the world.

"You alright?" Aurin asked.

Kara turned to Aurin and smiled as she answered, "Yeah. It's just a little strange without Delia around."

Delia had stayed behind in Khalia to take care of affairs and learn governance from her father. Kara on the other hand, had some promises she needed to keep. She also wanted to see the world before she left it for good.

"Delia's a big girl now. She needs to get out of her sister's shadow. It's a pretty big shadow." Aurin said.

"You trying to say I'm getting fat?" Kara joked.

Aurin laughed and asked, "Can goddesses even get fat?"

"Let's not find out."

The two headed into the city of Imbor. It was so different than the last time Kara had seen it. The city was vibrant and alive. People were running around with smiles on their faces. As people caught sight of her, cheers rang out in the streets. Some got on their knees in reverence. Others followed and reached out for her, hoping to feel the slight touch of the divine. Kara was still not used to all the love the people showed. She put a nervous smile on her face as she rode through the city towards her destination.

The people of Imbor had erected a monument towards the northern wall. It was in remembrance to the final defenders of Imbor. Kara got off her horse and approached the stone plaque. On the plaque was carved the names of all those who had fallen in the final moments of Anaya's freedom.

Kara ran her fingers across the plaque and found the name Nema. She remembered the brave Sarinan man who had taken command of the defenses when the people needed him. Kara ran down the list as she found Vima's name. The young boy had fought to the last, even though his arm had been cut off. Kara wiped the tears from her eyes as she thought of the courageous people of who stood with her that day.

Kara pulled a knife from her belt, the same one Vima had handed her before she left the city. He had given it to her as a piece of remembrance. She had promised to return to the city. She promised to liberate the people. As she looked around at all the smiling faces around her, she knew she had kept her promise.

Looking back down onto the plaque, Kara whispered, "I never forgot. I'll see you all soon."

A light flashed from Kara's hand as she burned the knife into the plaque. It would forever remain there as part of the monument. A symbol that their goddess would never forsake them and would always remember.

****

One year since wars end...

It had taken some time but the Numerans made good on their word. Slavery was officially abolished in Numera and outlawed throughout the world. Kara was in the capital city of Bella as Emperor Theodus made his speech to the people.

"The people of Numera have committed a horrible crime against their fellow man." Theodus began. "We acknowledge that we have done wrong in the past. We have attacked our neighbors, enslaved those less fortunate, and committed horrible crimes in the name of nationalism. No longer can we go on like this. We, the Numeran people, will accept responsibility and work to fix it. A small step in this will be taken today. From this day forward, slavery of another human being will forever be outlawed in our nation. May every man, woman, and child, be the masters of their own fate."

Kara didn't know whether the man truly believed the words coming out of his mouth. He had argued aggressively to keep slavery operational in Numera during the meeting. However, he wanted what was best for his nation. Kara couldn't fault him for that. If anything, Kara believed Numera was in the hands of a capable leader who could lead Numera into a future

The Goddess

that was better than before.

It shocked Kara to see the extent of the slavery that was present in Numera. As the slaves were freed, a mass exodus of people left the city, returning to their own homes. There were thousands of them. Smiling faces were everywhere as hope was renewed in their hearts. Long lost loved ones were reunited and journeyed together, back to their home lands. Kara was surprised to see that some chose to remain in Numera. Many slaves had been treated quite well by their masters and chose to remain as paid servants. There were quite a few women who were tasked with taking care of the children of certain families. These women had not been treated as slaves but as members of the family itself. They chose to remain and help raise the children rather than leave them. It dawned on Kara that even within a horrible institution like slavery, there was still some good to be had amongst the people.

As Kara made her way to the main square, she saw a sight that angered her. A memorial for General Bellus, adorned the middle of the square. It took every bit of Kara's self-restraint not to break it apart. As she approached it, the memorial was lined with flowers, precious jewels, incense, and adornments.

Kara stood there wondering how the Numerans could honor a war criminal when a woman came up beside her. She looked like an Anayan. She was holding a child, merely a few months old. The few strands of hair on the child's head looked darker than his mother's.

"I had to see it for myself." the woman said to Kara without taking her eyes off the monument.

Kara wondered if this woman was having the same feelings as her. Did she suffer under Bellus?

"He saved my life, you know." the woman said.

This surprised Kara. She was expecting the woman to say something negative about the monument and the man it was dedicated to.

"How?" Kara asked.

"I was a slave. I was assigned to the Emperor's throne. You

know what that means." the woman explained.

Kara knew well that it was a death sentence. Slaves that were assigned to the throne only lasted a few days at most before falling to exhaustion, at which point they were cruelly executed.

"Bellus pulled me out of that." the woman said.

"With all due respect, are you sure he didn't just want to use you?" Kara asked.

The woman chuckled and replied, "He preferred men."

"Oh!" Kara remarked.

This was something Kara had never expected. The Numerans considered such things a weakness. She was surprised Bellus had kept it a secret his entire life to become a general.

"He treated me well." the woman continued. "I was his slave. Instead, he treated me as a friend. Even offered to give me and my child a home after the war."

Kara began to reconsider her thoughts about the man. For the longest time, she'd looked upon Bellus as the enemy. She felt he was complicit in the crimes of his Emperor. This woman was saying something different.

"I was there you know." the woman said. "At the army camp in Khalia when you defeated the Emperor. Do you know how Bellus died?"

Kara had known the Emperor had killed Bellus. She assumed it was because the Emperor felt his general had failed him.

"When you came off that cross and began to slaughter the Numerans, Emperor Gradus ordered the men forward. Bellus refused to do so." the woman explained. "He stood up to the Emperor at the risk of his own life in order to protect his men. He cared for them so much. That is why this memorial is here. The people honor him because he gave his own life for them."

Kara was at a loss for words. She had no idea about any of this.

The woman went over to the foot of the memorial. She placed a worn spoon onto the stone plaque. Kara didn't know

The Goddess

the significance of the spoon, but she could tell it was important to the woman. Although Bellus was not there, Kara had a feeling it was important to the general as well.

"I ask you goddess, for my sake, please don't forget my friend." the woman told Kara before turning back to memorial again. "Goodbye, Bellus. I love you, old friend."

As the woman left, Kara went closer to the memorial. She used her hand to burn the spoon into the plaque, the same way she had done to the knife in Imbor.

Kara placed her hand on the monument and said, "General Bellus, I've always thought of you as an enemy. Maybe if we had met, I could've seen you as something more. Know that the gates to my kingdom will not be closed to you. I look forward to meeting you when I get there."

Aurin came up to Kara, handing her a cup of tea. The man had insisted on coming with her on her trip to see the world, but he was never around anymore. He would run off and leave Kara to do her own thing. Strangely, Kara missed having him tag along everywhere she went.

"Where to now?" Aurin asked.

"I think I'm ready to go home." Kara answered.

****

Fourteen months after wars end...

Kara stood in her room, looking at the mess in front of her. She had worn the same armor for over a year now. Apparently, goddesses don't stink over time and didn't need a change of clothes. Yet, her room was still a mess for some reason. Kara chuckled as she wondered what her room in her kingdom would look like. Jophiel had said that she never changed so Kara assumed she'd always been a messy deity.

It was time to say goodbye. Her work here was done, and it was up to everyone else to make this world their own. It was sad to go. She had spent the past twenty-four years growing up in this room. As Kara reached the door, she turned back one last time and smiled.

"Goodbye, room."

Kara reached the main throne room to see her family gathered there, her father, Gallus, Miru, Aurin, and Delia. They knew this was the day she would be leaving them. They all had tears in their eyes.

Miru stepped up and took Kara's hands.

"I don't know if I should bow to you or give you a hug." Miru said.

Kara smiled and embraced the old man.

"I'll settle for a hug." Kara said. "You might be the archbishop, but you'll always be my family."

King Atlin came over and embraced his daughter tightly. He didn't want to let go but knew Kara would be going to a better place.

"I love you, sweet girl." the king said as he wiped the tears from his eyes.

Kara smiled at her father and said, "I love you, father. I'll tell mother you said hi."

General Gallus came up afterwards and hugged Kara with a smile.

"Goodbye, uncle Gallus." Kara said.

It was the best gift Gallus could've wished for, to hear Kara call him uncle one last time.

Kara moved over to Aurin who was in tears. The man still had a smile on his face. His friend and charge was leaving again. This time, she wasn't coming back. However, Aurin also had no doubts as to where she was going.

"I love you, Aurin. Thank you for all the years you've been with me." Kara told him.

The two embraced but Aurin couldn't find the words to say. It was unnecessary anyway. Kara already knew how the man felt.

Finally, there was Delia. The brave warrior princess and heir to the throne of Khalia was weeping like a child.

"Do you have to go?" Delia asked.

Kara could help but shed some tears as she looked upon

her beloved sister. Kara embraced the girl and whispered into her ear, "I will always be with you."

As the two parted, Delia softly said, "I love you."

"I love you, Delia. You will be a great queen."

Kara made her way outside the doors of the royal palace, her family behind her. The entire city had shown up to bid their goddess farewell. The entire city knelt at once and bowed their heads, not only in reverence but in appreciation for all that Kara had done for them.

Kara looked back and smiled at her family one last time. With a brilliant flash of light, the goddess was gone from the world. Instead of feeling empty, the people felt hope. Kara had created a better world and handed it over to them. They knew their goddess watched over them and they were determined to make her proud.

****

Thus, the story of Kara, reincarnation of Yalka, goddess to not only Khalia but the people of the world, ends. I have recorded these events to the best of my abilities from my own experiences and those who were there. The goddess herself saw these writings but I leave it to the reader to decide whether she liked it or not. However, the smile on her face as she read my work seemed to indicate a certain favor.

Kara did not come to this world to fight a simple war. She came to teach its people a lesson. It would have been easy for her to be born privileged and respected from the start. Instead, she persevered against hate, fear, and uncertainty. She led by example so that we may live our lives as she did.

So, I write these words, that future generations may benefit and know the truth of what happened here. Who am I, you may ask? I am Breka, once stable boy to the royal family, now royal guard to Princess Delia.

ABOUT THE AUTHOR

Dave R.H. is a writer of several different genres. Dave has experience in programming with a focus on game development. In his spare time, he enjoys video games and movies which have a deep and impactful story. His goal is to one day apply his skills to writing for a game development company. He currently resides in New Jersey with his family.

Copyright © 2019 Dave R.H.
All rights reserved.

Made in the USA
Middletown, DE
08 April 2019